A Heart

ACROSS *the* OCEAN

ALSO BY SHELLEY KASSIAN

Contemporary Romance

Places in the Heart:

A Sea for Summer, Book 1

A Mountain Leads Home, Book 2

The Thurston Hotel:

A Lasting Harmony, Book 5

The Women of Stampede:

The Half Mile of Baby Blue, Book 2

Historical Romance

A Sacrifice for Love

A Gentleman for Christmas

Shelley Kassian writing as Abby Lane

Dark Fantasy

A Reign of Blood and Magic:

The Scarlett Mark, Book 1

The Ebony Queen, Book 2

The Immortal Blood, Book 3

A Heart ACROSS the OCEAN

A Novel

SHELLEY KASSIAN

—A Heart across the Ocean—

Published 2018 by Shelley Kassian
(shelleykassian.com)

ISBN: 978-0-9959680-4-2 (Print edition)
ISBN: 978-0-9959680-3-5 (Kindle edition)
ISBN: 978-0-9959680-2-8 (Other digital edition)

Design and cover art by Su Kopil, Earthly Charms
Copyediting by Ted Williams

DEDICATION

*I dedicate my fifth novel to the love of my life,
my husband, Wayne.
When I met him during my grade 11 year at high school,
I recognized my love for him almost from the start.
Years later, it's clear we're soulmates.
Swans swimming beside each other.
Hearts from across the Ocean.*

FOREWORD

Shake hands with a bit of Canadian history as Ms. Kassian takes her readers along on Madeleine's grueling ocean crossing to New France where Madeleine is expected to marry a total stranger. Shocking secrets and ulterior motives abound in this historical tale of a dangerous new land where death awaits the unwary. But amid the uncertainty and fears, finding love is always a possibility.

Brenda Sinclair, author of the contemporary Carsen Family Trilogy: *Tangled Heartstrings, Tangled Memories,* and *Tangled Intentions.*

PREFACE

A Heart across the Ocean was written to commemorate Canada's 150th birthday. The story is meant to pay tribute to the King's daughters (filles du Roi), Parisian women who immigrated to New France between the years of 1663 and 1673, to marry colonists or officers from the Carignan-Salière's regiment.

While Canada celebrated its 150th birthday on July 1, 2017, the French history of Canada has existed since Jacques Cartier discovered a native land in 1535. The best part of writing this novel has been learning the history of French Canadians, aboriginal people, and some 800 brave women. Many descendants can trace their genealogy to the *filles du Roi*, which is why they have become known in modern times as Founding Mothers.

The initiative of sending women to Canada came from King Louis XIV and was supported by Jean Talon, Intendant of New France from 1665 to 1668 and 1669 to 1672, mainly to grow the colony. Filles du Roi were screened to ensure they were free to marry and of an age appropriate for giving birth.

Early in my research, I learned that many women, perhaps as many as one-third or one-half, came from the Hôpital Général, or its female annex, the Salpêtrière in Paris. More an institution than a hospital, it accommodated orphans, indigents, prostitutes, and those suffering from poverty or misfortune. Some notable men of the period claimed that *filles de joie*, or prostitutes, may have immigrated to New France, too. Historians have disputed these claims. This knowledge impacted the premise of this novel.

The truth lies buried in history. I chose to believe that the filles du Roi were brave women traveling to the new world to begin a new life, birthing a legacy for their descendants.

I hope you enjoy *A Heart across the Ocean*.
Shelley Kassian

ACKNOWLEDGMENTS

I thank my colleagues, Brenda Sinclair and Katie O'Connor for beta reading this book prior to publication. Their advice contributed to the plot, further developing the story. Acting on their suggestions, I added a bit more internal thought and blue-penciled one scene, likely saving me one or two: "Why did you do that?" reviews.

Thanks to Su Kopil for designing an awesome cover! Every time I look at this one, I really get the feel of the heroine, Madeleine.

Thanks to Ted Williams for his editing expertise, which brings continuity to the manuscript. I especially appreciate his attention to French spellings and his knowledge of language.

Finally, I thank my family who always support my publishing efforts! They share my Facebook posts, indulge my story ideas, and spare me the time to do what I enjoy best. Write!

CHAPTER 1

DIEPPE, FRANCE

May 1666

Madeleine Bourbonnais had accepted this new compass bearing in her life, despite her fears of finding a husband and the ocean voyage to New France. Once decisions were made, fate could not escape its guilty charge.

"I see what you're thinking," the night watchman barked, hurrying Madeleine across a cobblestoned wharf to a waiting ship. "Quit your thoughts of escape. They'll naught get you anywhere fast."

"You ugly and cruel human being!" she shouted, sneering at the beast of a man. "How could you comprehend my turmoil, or the worry hurting my head? Your cruel grip, forcing me against my will to a place I've never seen before, and the crossing I must cope with to arrive on a distant shore.

Unhand me, Monsieur. I'll go with you, obeying the orders of a king whose only purpose in this scheme is to rid the Parisian streets of poverty and crime."

"Ungrateful wench, how dare you criticize our monarch, or me for that matter. Shush your ill mouth and let me do my job."

"Your job is inhumane," she exclaimed, stopping for a breath and straining against his handgrip. "Capturing orphans from rat-infested streets. Locking up the innocent and those down on their luck with, with the ill at heart? Only a cruel man would confine harmless citizens in such a place."

"You're not an innocent, but I'll admit it," he grunted, pausing in his step to study her face. "Human solutions to poverty cannot right every wrong, but lucky for you, Sister Constance achieved a husbandly scheme to benefit your situation."

The nun had made the voyage possible, insisting that a kind and loving God never challenged a human soul with more grief than one could manage. In Madeleine's estimation, the nun was wrong. A woman required skills stronger than her faith to overcome troubles, and she could not see any hope or love in this decision. How could the avowal of a husband, *if a man sought her hand,* change anything?

"I accepted the offer to free myself of confinement. There was no other choice but to take King Louis's dowry and travel to New France. I don't really want to go, two and a half months at sea? What woman would willingly accept such a fate?"

"True enough. Most women would not travel to relieve themselves of difficulty," Simon Legrand said with a smirk, his grip relaxing. "But men, eh, and travel on the high seas, what an adventure that could be."

Madeleine's gatekeeper appeared wistful. She preferred his reserve as he led her forward, ushering her through a throng of people. *What could she say? Accept her fate?* She had little choice but to tread the port of Dieppe's grand quay attempting to retain her dignity.

Holding her head high, she was led past other wayfarers. Sailors whistled, catcalled, or winked provocatively. Freshly polished in a new mulberry gown, she cringed, enduring the sexual innuendo, having received such requests before. She much preferred the ogling of fishermen who pushed iron-wheeled carts full of gudgeon, grayling, or dace. Coupled with the misted sea air that seemed especially gray this morning, the forthcoming journey was equally dire. Sighing, she swallowed her fears.

"Look around. You should give notice to these men's desires," Simon said, squeezing her arm. "Isn't the king's optioning a better fate?"

"How will the acceptance of yet another man's hand change anything? Not that you would care, but ten weeks at sea—how will I tolerate the crossing?"

"I've heard sailors sharing their seafaring tales over a pint, revealing that their journeys across the Atlantic are long, arduous, and cold. But a woman like you," he said with a sneer, "your bed is sure to be warm."

Madeleine winced, shivering, clutching a carpetbag to her side. She swallowed her anger, choosing silence while reflecting on the practical items she had brought with her: a bonnet, a taffeta handkerchief, stockings, gloves, ribbon, and shoelaces. Items for stitchery, including white thread, needles, pins, and scissors. All provided through the king's dowry. Madeleine Bourbonnais, *a fille du Roi, a King's daughter,* she must accept this opportunity to find a husband as it came with fringe benefits. But she would not accept the sailors' catcalls or the nasty intercourse to which this man referred.

"You're a heartless human being," Madeleine blurted, pausing on the wharf, shrugging, trying to escape his cincture on her arm.

"Your opinion hardly matters to me. I call it the way I see it. Accept who you are and quit your trouble."

"Bâtard!"

Indifferent, he yanked her forward, bringing her closer to the galleon, *and her destiny,* weaving among a busy barrage of men and women, children, too. To distract her attention, *from fear, from worry,* she glanced at the ocean, smelling the salty brine, watching the seagulls stretch their wings in flight, listening to their screech and wondering if escape was possible from this change in her life.

"Vive la France!" she muttered under her breath, shaking her head. "I shall never return to these rat-infested streets. The ship is in sight; you may release me, Monsieur. Yes?"

She pulled away from his grasp, pleading. "You nasty piece of fish bait, I'll not try to run. Unhand me, Monsieur! Let me go. You've taken me far enough, and though I've accepted my fate, my passage, I'm not a sheep to be led to the slaughter."

"Don't be dramatic. My instructions were to escort you to the ship. You're not to return to the streets of Paris. Sister Constance gave me explicit instructions."

"As if I'd ever want to return to such filth." Madeleine winced, reminded of unpleasant experiences on the streets of misfortune. "I've not found sympathy or compassion from the people who frequent the streets of Paris. Neither, mind you, have I found much kindness from the pitiful asylum you fetched me from."

He smiled at her, grinning something obscene.

"I see where your thoughts lie, Monsieur. I know what you're thinking."

"Mais oui? You can read my mind?"

"You have an indecent opinion of the women at the Hôpital, at Salpêtrière. They're not ladies of the night. That nonsense could not be further from the truth."

"Women down on their luck?" he asked, snickering, his brows rising in question. "Please, do not humor me with more lies. I know the look. I see the girls who live at the hospital. I fetched many of them from the streets myself. You included!"

He winked and licked his lips as if to imply he knew more than she. *Idiot. Fiend!* She hated men like him.

"Imbecile. How dare you make such insinuations! Women cannot be judged based on the clothing they wear, or the rouge applied to their cheeks." Madeleine fumed, pausing on the dock, straining against his grasp. "Surely, you don't believe I'm a woman of a shameful nature? I'm an orphan, Monsieur."

"An orphan?" he sniggered. She flinched when he pinched her derriere. "Bah! I'd entertain your good graces myself," he boasted, clucking his tongue, "if not for the disease you'd mark me with!"

"Oh—" Madeleine scoffed, turning up her nose. "That's an ugly sentiment to express to a lady."

"Madam, you're in denial. I don't understand why Sister Constance has such faith in you. Sending you to the new world to turn an officer's head with, with the itch? Seems wrong to engage an honest man with a woman who will only bring him sorrow."

"Sorrow? How dare you, Monsieur." She was so angry, hot tears blinded her eyesight. She was a fool to think that this man, *or any man, frankly*, would regard her kindly. "I'll hear no more of your slanderous words."

"I'd rather not listen to more falsehoods myself, my Lady," he exaggerated, leading her to the gangplank. "Come this way."

"Hmph!" Madeleine huffed, straining against his hold, climbing the gangplank, soon meeting the ship's captain. She gazed longingly at the cobbled walk below, missing her homeland already, feeling the ship's sway even though it was moored, seeing it was useless to run. He would only catch her again.

"Simon Legrand, you've shepherded another fille du Roi to the ship?"

"I have, Captain."

Madeleine breathed a sigh of relief when the night watchman released his hold on her arm.

"Ah, yes," Simon said, motioning to her, "make way for the king's daughter. One more woman traveling to New France with the benefit of a dowry; fifty livres bestowed on her person from our own country's treasury. Captain François, allow me to introduce to you, Madeleine Bourbonnais."

"Enchanté, Mademoiselle," he articulated, bowing from the neck. "Welcome aboard the Saint-Jean Baptiste, my seaworthy galleon."

"Merci, Captain," Madeleine replied, grateful for his show of respect.

"I leave this woman in your care. I must return to Paris. Perhaps, I'll find more pretty girls to send to the new world."

"His insinuations are not true, I'm not *that* type of woman, Captain."

"I wish you safe passage across the Atlantic, Madeleine Bourbonnais, should that be your real name. For regardless of your true nature, if you survive the long journey, you'll toil for the rest of your days."

"Good riddance, you godless swine."

"Adieu to you, too. I'm not unkind. I do hope you find a suitable husband."

Madeleine sighed, then watched the wretch stomp down the gangplank and disappear into a sea of people.

"The man seems certain of his opinions," the captain muttered, looking at her with a studious expression. "Pay no mind to men such as him. Having witnessed the darker side of life, he's forgotten a part of his own humanity."

"If he was ever in touch with his soul," she said, turning, gazing at the other women coming on board the ship.

"Pierre?" The captain appealed to a crew member. "Show Mademoiselle Bourbonnais where to stow her bag." He sought her attention again. "After this day, you begin a new life. Get ready, we soon set sail for La Rochelle and from that port, we depart to New France, where your husband awaits your attention."

"If any man will accept my hand."

The captain stepped toward her, grasped her chin and gently tipped her face to his inspection. "You'll be wanted. A beauty such as you will have several men courting your attention. You'll be wed and giving birth to a tiny blessing of the New World before you know it."

"Wed and…"

"Don't look so frightened. This is the reason you travel to New France. To grow the colony."

"Yes," Madeleine replied, staring at the wharf, the blue waters, and contemplating the distance across the ocean. She could not change her past, but maybe some good could be found in her future.

MADELEINE CONSIDERED LEAVING the ship when the Saint-Jean sailed into the port of La Rochelle. But the captain's kindness kept her on board, standing at the railing, her linen skirt wafting in the breeze, watching as more king's daughters, women bound for the French colony, came on board the ship.

You'll be wanted… She hoped so.

A well-dressed woman sauntered toward Madeleine, wearing a bright pink gown with a cream woolen shawl draped around her shoulders. A beauty, chocolate wisps of hair escaped her bonnet and nut-brown eyes sparkled with intrigue.

"Bonjour," she blurted, a beautiful smile on her rouged face.

The inflection in her tone either expressed her happiness

or hid her disquiet. Madeleine could not be sure. "Marie, Marie Chauvet," the woman said, extending a white-gloved hand.

"Madeleine." She grasped Marie's fingers momentarily, guarded from the start.

"Lovely to meet you, Madeleine. Are you a king's daughter?"

"Yes, I am."

"Me, too." She giggled, pressing closer. "I suppose all the women onboard the vessel are wards of the king. Madeleine, if you wish it, we could be fast friends. We might need each other's companionship, friendship, and support during the long journey to New France, yes? Perhaps once we make land, too. Especially if love does not flourish?"

"I don't expect to find love." Madeleine confessed, staring at the sea. "My needs are simpler and more pressing. I require a husband."

"Oh, you do? Whatever for?" she asked, staring at Madeleine intently, causing her cheeks to flush with guilt.

"Whatever for?" Madeleine replied, swallowing. "It's the king's wish I wed, to assist with advancing the needs of the colony."

"Of course! But surely you have greater cause to cross the Atlantic than to marry a man."

"We've only just met, Marie."

"Oh, does my conversation make you uncomfortable? I could speak to someone else if you'd rather be left alone."

"No, it's not that, it's…"

"You're not ready to share the true reason," Marie whispered, stepping nearer, "it's too uncomfortable?"

"Yes," Madeleine admitted, not meeting her eyes.

"I've seen apprehension like this before. Perhaps—if you don't mind me saying—there might be another reason?"

Madeleine didn't say anything. Turning away, she escaped the conversation and walked to the handrail, but the woman named Marie followed her. "It's all right, you don't have to tell me anything."

Marie scanned the proximity of other passengers who might overhear their conversation, then grasped Madeleine's arm and led her to the quarterdeck. "You can trust me, Madeleine. Whatever your truth, your confidence is safe with me. Every woman has her secrets, after all. God only knows, how I've kept mine."

CHAPTER 2

VILLE DE QUÉBEC, NEW FRANCE

A shrouded halo of light hung low in the sky, its glow barely visible through the clouds on the eastern horizon. The hour was early; the Carignan-Salières officers had barely risen from their bunks, but a few men rushed across the courtyard, making their way to the mess hall, ready to carry out their military duties for the day. Julian had abandoned his lodgings early, not wanting to speak to his commanding officer. He knew a lecture was forthcoming, perhaps a verbal warning, too.

Another miserable and cold spring day, he mused as he walked across the courtyard, disliking the weeping rain. He had yet to witness the sun this week, and he yearned for the light to return. As he walked, he fought against the chill and the bristling wind nipping at his cheeks. He pulled his woolen collar tighter to the nape of his neck, hating the bitter cold in this new world. A bitch of a day, the wetness chilled him to the bone. He shivered. He'd never grow accustomed to this rugged place regardless of its wild beauty and fresh clean air. He missed the comforts of home and family, and France.

Reaching for the door handle to the commander's quarters, begrudgingly, Julian stepped inside. A gentle fire burned inside the hearth. He removed his slouch hat, holding it in his hands. Sitting comfortably at his desk, René dropped his papers on the desktop.

"Thank you for coming so promptly."

Julian placed his hat on the coat rack, followed by his brown long-coat. Walking to the fireplace, he massaged his hands near the flames in an attempt at warmth.

"You gave me little choice in the matter. So here I am at your command."

"We have several matters to discuss. The least of which, your refusal to take a wife."

"There's that," Julian groaned, turning to René. "I didn't expect you to get to the point so quickly."

"What's holding you back? You've made your promises to king and country to protect this new land. You've taken up your duty with a degree of temerity that's been well documented on your military record, to the credit of your company. But you refuse to submit to one simple ideal, which our intendant Talon and our king hold dear."

Julian walked to a chair positioned across from the desk and sat. "Honestly, René, these conversations grow tiresome. We've discussed the subject at length. I have a girl waiting for me at home. When I finish my tour of duty, I'll return to France and take Catherine as my bride."

"New France requires your service for two more years. But never mind that, if the woman had any love of you, she'd have already crossed the Atlantic Ocean." René emphasized, tapping a quill on the desk. "Children are required in the womb of this new world. Such material gain cannot be reaped unless an officer has a place to stow his position. Talon has said as much himself."

"With all due respect, Sir, I'm shocked you would insinuate that Catherine has no heart. It's a sacrifice to come to this godforsaken land. I don't expect my girl to leave her life for me. And as for Talon—"

"Look, when you came to this country, you asked her to come with you. She refused. You've been here a year. You made the sacrifice; why can't the woman you profess to love have the same heart?"

"I'm a man, René. I don't expect Catherine to cross an ocean for me. The journey is long and difficult. She promised to wait until I completed my tour of duty. I tried to understand her decision."

"You cannot admit the truth, but regardless, the king won't let you wait. He has sent brave women to build this colony, and you have been complacent too long. Captain Benoit, we lead by example, so be an example to your men."

"As I recall, my role in the military empowers more than management and duty. I ensure the sentries are at their posts to guard against attacks, manage the patrols, and keep a watchful eye for the native warriors who might be lurking in the forest. I *submit* to my duty. The king should not expect any of his officers to blindly marry women fresh off the boat."

René dropped his quill in obvious exasperation, puffing a

sigh. "Be careful who you share your regards with. The king's rulings are notable. Directives should be recognized and adhered to. A ship is expected to make port in a few weeks, and the women on board are arriving especially for the officers of New France. When the boat docks, *if* your past love interest is not standing on the ship's deck, your new love will wait on your affections."

"The king and Talon are crazy to have devised this scheme."

"I beg to differ, Julian. We need our young men to remain in New France, and these boys require wives if they are to stay and build their futures. I expect you to fall in line, like the others."

"What are you saying?"

"Don't make me angry. You have stalled long enough. Take a wife and reap the benefits. They are yours to receive."

"The officers' bribe won't pressure me; you cannot make me commit."

"Two hundred livres is not a small sum to cast aside, not to mention, I could grant you a seigneury—a plot of land—a home to build on it and more besides."

"I don't want these things. I want to return to France, to Catherine."

"Julian, you misunderstand. I'm done with your excuses. I command you to take a wife. When the king's daughters arrive at port, I expect you to greet them. This will give you time to appraise each girl, *taking in the possibilities*, which could assist with embracing a prospect."

"I'll do as you command, I'll see to their arrival, to their safety, but…"

"But nothing!" René yelled, his voice stern, his cheeks reddening. "Forget this woman, this Catherine. 'Tis my duty to see that the king's commands are met; my responsibility to ensure you act in accordance with His Majesty's directives, and if you don't comply, there will be a penalty for your refusal."

"René—" Julian blew up, angering. "This is an injustice. You cannot—"

René stood. Tall, he came to Julian, towering above him. Scowling, his tense expression delivered a warning.

"No more refusals. When the ship arrives, you have one day to select three viable options for a bride." He waved his index finger. "A second day to shorten the list to one lady. On the third day, you'll sign a marriage contract with your prospective bride. And then, you shall be married."

"If I refuse?"

"If you refuse?" The commander smiled, slyly. "I will choose your bride. Carry you bodily to the altar if I must. Can you imagine sleeping with a woman who your commanding officer has chosen? One might think you would have the common sense to do the choosing yourself."

Julian understood by the spit flying from his commander's mouth that his chances of escaping this order were lessening. "You would do that to me?"

"I give you the option of a king's daughter, or a tribunal. I would think that saying: '*I do*,' would be the lesser of the two evils, and more pleasurable by far."

"Hmph," Julian responded, huffing. "You leave me no other choice. It's a bastard of a deal."

"Are you coming to your senses, you'll meet the ship?"

He rose from the armchair and retreated from the commander, walking to the door. "I'll meet the ship."

"Don't look so downtrodden. The nights are cold, they'll be sweeter with a woman to warm your bed."

He gathered his hat and coat. "Have a good day, René."

"Your compliance warms my heart. Besides the seigneury, I'll gift your marriage with a suckling pig and a half-dozen chickens for good measure."

Outfitted for the journey into the rain, Julian reached for the door handle, disregarding the remuneration, but then an idea came to him. He confronted his commander, again.

"I'll expect your company on the shoreline, your hand nearby, too. As you say, the king has his rules and together, we shall make an impression to build the colony. Sacrifices should be shared."

"Is that what it will take?"

"It will make the pain easier to accept."

"Alert me when the ship arrives, we'll meet at the harbor. Take this adventure together? The nights do grow tiresome, and cold. I must confess; I miss the banter of a lady's conversation."

"I'm sure you do."

Julian shook his head and escaped into the rain.

Catherine, I'm sorry.

LATER THAT NIGHT, Julian sat at his writing desk. By the wavering glow of a tallow candle, he considered what words to write. *What should he say?* He knew this letter would bring Catherine pain. But René was right. She would not come to New France. She had refused his repeated requests, and this new world needed him. He would not disappoint his commanding officer, his men, or the king for that matter.

He finally scribed:

Dear Catherine,

I hope this letter finds you well. There's no easy way to tell you what needs to be said, so I'll confide the truth. I have decided to stay in New France and build a life for myself here. And—In order to assist with building the colony, I have been asked to take a wife.

He held the feather quill in his hand. The ink pooled on the tip and dripped to the paper, forming an indigo stain on the parchment. Taking on the impression of a tiny tear-stain, the mark seemed appropriate.

I want to assure you, I did not make this decision lightly. If you must know, the king made it for me. I will not have you wait for a future that is impossible. Forget me, Catherine. It appears the two of us were not meant to be. Take a husband. Birth many children. Have a happy life.

All my best,

—Julian.

CHAPTER 3

The Saint-Jean Baptiste cut through the waves at a good clip. The galleon sailed through a moderate current, rising and falling with the swell of the sea, her masts flapping with the wind and spray shooting over the bow. The wooden ship lurched back and forth—continually heaving upward and sinking beneath the wave troughs. Madeleine swayed on the deck, her legs weak, her stomach unsettled, *churning*. She stared at the whitecaps on the water, mindful of land that waited on a distant shore.

What man waits for me in New France? What will he think when he learns my secret? The truth of her situation could wait. Nine more weeks of seasickness must be endured, first.

Swallowing, she tried to calm the rising angst that prompted illness after only one week at sea. She wasn't successful. She wavered on her feet, hastening across the deck to a pail, plunging to her knees and losing her breakfast.

Madeleine felt a pressure on her shoulder. She turned to

see who had touched her, soon contemplating the captain and his sea-blue eyes.

"The voyage southwest is always difficult," he said, scrutinizing her face with concern. "The seas are choppy today and I don't imagine the wind will let up anytime soon. Perhaps it's best to return to your quarters?"

Madeleine drew in a shaky breath, wiping at her mouth, lowering her gaze. "Remaining inside the cabin is worse," she mumbled, swallowing again. "A hole in the shadows? At least on deck the breeze and the salty air seem to help."

"Are you getting enough fluids? Dehydration has led many souls to a watery grave."

"I'm having difficulty keeping anything down, fluids or solid food."

Her stomach heaved, and she leaned toward the pail in response. Once she finished, François helped her rise to her feet and then led her away from the bow.

"Madeleine, when on deck, stay on the quarterdeck and on the leeward side, downwind. Look to the horizon, not the swaying of the ship. It might help."

"Nothing will help."

"Don't despair. It's clear you're not the seafaring type, but there's always hope you'll develop sea legs. I have faith you'll grow accustomed to the rocking."

"I hope so."

"Permit me to do something for you," he said with a grin, his expression comforting. "I'll have the cook offer a spare ration to help settle your stomach. Perhaps extra hardtack for the evening meal?"

"Kind of you to consider my needs." Madeleine belched,

not excited about the heavy wafer. The thought of biting into an unappetizing foodstuff caused another wave of illness, but gratefully, she squashed it down. "I'd be grateful for anything that might help."

Marie, having become a companion on this journey, strolled nearer when the captain stepped away. She pressed close. "Hardtack will not help what ails you, young miss."

"Please…" Madeleine begged, fearful that someone might overhear Marie's statement. Somehow, her new friend had guessed the truth.

"Oh, don't worry," Marie replied, whispering in her ear, leaning close, taking her arm and ushering her to the aft area. "Your secret is safe with me. After all, we all have confidences to keep safe."

Madeleine acknowledged her admission, swaying with the ocean and mindful that Marie kept her skeletons well buried.

MARIE PRESSED close to Madeleine's side as they walked past several women who had come on deck during the troublesome weather. Madeleine understood why. It was terrifying being housed in the hold, in a perpetual black night without the benefit of a lit candle. Candles were not permitted for fear of fire, so the ladies tolerated the choppy seas above decks, rather than being confined inside the shadows.

Grateful for the distraction, she reflected on the other filles du Roi, twenty-four women from different social classes. She wondered if they cared about her illness or if they believed the swells caused the sensitivity. Or perhaps they didn't care she was sick.

"How far along are you, Mademoiselle?" Marie whispered, pressing closer.

"'Tis hard to know, but I think the days are early."

"Can you feel the flutter of a butterfly's wings within your belly?"

"I beg your pardon?"

Marie glanced at her tummy. "The seed resting beneath your pillow?"

"Oh, no, I'm unaware of any such movement."

"Perhaps weeks then, but by the time we arrive in New France, the first stirrings of life will be noticeable. By you and others, which means…"

"I must hide the truth," Madeleine responded, swallowing, glancing away, ashamed of her situation.

"You cannot hide your sins away forever. These problems have a way of growing, but don't worry. Women before you have borne the pangs of burden and women after you will, too."

A daughter strolled nearer. "Hmm," she muttered, assessing them. "What are the two of you discussing in your little tête-à-tête?"

"Mademoiselle Louise," Marie acknowledged with a nervous giggle, "it's kind of you to ask. After all, Madeleine has been ill."

"It hardly appeared that you were conversing about her health."

"And wise you are, too, to see the truth. Isn't it obvious?

We contemplate the pleasure that awaits us in New France. Our futures; our husbands."

Marie winked at Madeleine, licking her lower lip, offering a simpering smile as if some conspiracy might soon take place. She stepped closer to Louise and whispered something in her ear.

"Madame!" Louise chided, placing her hands on her hips. "You are rude! I cannot believe a gentle born lady would voice such a sentiment."

"Don't be a prude," Marie retorted, quicker than was wise, proud of her moral compass. "Louise, do you dream of a husband to share your bed? The pleasure awaiting you in the bedchamber of the new world?"

"I'm pledged to marry. I will not burden myself with the luxury of carnality, or love. Such a happenstance is unlikely."

"At your age, I would have to agree."

"Mademoiselle Marie," she said with a huff, her face flaming red. "Did your mother not teach you any manners?"

"She taught me to find a suitable husband before I reached an age where bearing children would be impossible."

"Marie," Madeleine beseeched, touching Marie's arm. "Perhaps we should not irritate our older sister."

"Respect is offered where respect is due."

"What do you know of respect? You have no consideration; no manners either," Louise complained, obviously offended.

A daughter sidestepped toward them as the ship rose on another swell, soon plunging, again. Shy, she could not meet their eyes, and kept looking anywhere but at Marie.

"I, ah," she began, "would like to believe love is possible?"

Madeleine swallowed, fearing the churning sensation inside her stomach. She indicated with her fluttering hand she could not talk. Unwell, she staggered to the railing and heaved bile into the sea. Marie was soon beside her.

"Poor dear," she said, rubbing her back. "I hope this sea illness lets up soon, or the journey ahead will be dreadful."

Madeleine suppressed the pangs, wiped at her mouth, then ambled toward the young woman. "What is your name?" she asked.

"Geneviève," the pretty young woman replied. Madeleine reflected on the amethyst color of her eyes.

"I'm sorry to burst your bubble, Geneviève, but it has been my experience that the ambitions of men are more apt to rise and fall like the waves on the sea. A plundering if you will. Fickle, they are. Wanting only the briefest moment of a woman's time, and only for their self-serving needs or further amusement. Geneviève, most men cannot be trusted."

"You seem well-educated on the matter," Louise ground out, stepping nearer. "What do you know of a man's nature?"

"Only that which I have been forced to beg for, in order to survive."

"Were you an orphan?" Geneviève asked, a coy expression on her face.

"I spent some time on the streets."

"She's a prostitute." Louise snarled, her hands on her hips. "And she looks the type."

"You horrible woman." Madeleine scolded the harpy, stepping forward and stopping so close to Louise's face, she could see the whites of her steel-gray eyes. "How dare you say such a thing. For all your upper-class morals, you speak of someone you do not know with a callous disregard."

Unafraid, Louise stood her ground, twirling white pearls at the nape of her neck, in the act stating both a superior attitude and that her point was correct. "'Tis the truth, is it not?"

"You would not recognize the truth if it struck you in the face. And it could, if you're not careful."

"Madame demimonde, the air is foul with your breathing. Get out of my way."

Madeleine could not bear to have the ugly term thrown in her face. She reached for the woman's throat and thrust her to the ground. Louise screamed when her head slammed against the ship's decking.

"Get off me," she shrieked, twisting to and fro, "you murderous creature!"

Madeleine gripped Louise's shoulders, and then pulled her upward, thrusting her against the deck. "Don't speak ill of me. I won't hesitate to throw you overboard if you're ever rude or unkind to me again."

"Stop!" Louise shouted, slapping at her face, punching her chest. "I will not have your venomous hands on my body."

"Now ladies, settle down," Captain François called to them, rushing forward and soon breaking them apart with the assistance of two crew members. "No murderous intent on board the ship. This mainstay is too cramped for quarrels."

"Trollop!" Louise yelled. She rose to her feet with the assistance of a sailor's hand, rubbing bright red finger marks on her neck.

"You best observe my warning." Madeleine threatened

Louise, her face smarting. "I will not tolerate your name calling, you insolent woman."

"Take Madeleine to the galley," the captain said with a frown.

She had made a mistake that would mark her for the rest of her voyage at sea. She stood on the deck, her skirts swaying with the breeze, feeling very much alone while the other women gathered around the old girl and ushered her into their confidence.

They stared, choosing a side. Sabine, Jeanne, and many more women whose names she did not know. They judged her behavior, past and present. And poor Geneviève wore an expression of abject horror.

Shame suffused Madeleine's cheeks, the heat staining her face. Not an admission of guilt, but her weakness succeeded in shaping a humorless smile on Louise's lips. Madeleine considered saying she was sorry, but couldn't bring herself to apologize.

Marie's hand squeezed her elbow. "Come, Madeleine," Marie said, beckoning her to leave the situation while wearing a bemused expression. "The air in the aft section is suddenly stale with disregard."

EVEN THOUGH THE confrontation with Louise Bercier was over, the resulting anxiety only served to upset Madeleine further. She became so sick she was soon dry heaving. The ship's surgeon had given her laudanum to help her sleep. It was night now. Dark. Pitch black in the ship's hold.

Madeleine could not see her hand in front of her face while lying inside the bunk. When Marie pressed closer, she was grateful for her warmth. The damp cold seeped into the cramped space they shared with several other girls. Fully dressed, too cold to remove their clothing, they shared two woolen blankets to keep warm.

Madeleine grew accustomed to Marie's breathing tickling the nape of her neck. Having a warm body nestled close to her was a comfort and the only way to stay warm. But with Marie pressed near, the shivers racked her body and she yearned for a blazing fire. But other than the brick fireplace in the galley, fire onboard ship was strictly forbidden.

"I'm so cold," she said with a yawn, fighting the medicine lulling her to dream. "Marie, if not for your warmth…"

Marie pressed closer. "Did you mean what you said?" she asked, concern in her voice.

"What's that?"

"That a man cannot be trusted?"

"In my experience, men are the worst type of scum."

"You've been with a man. 'Tis obvious. Who might the father be?"

"The father?" Madeleine sighed, not wanting to remember. "He only desired his pleasure. A hold to stow his…"

"Affection?" Marie asked. "But what of the man? Was he handsome? Did he touch you gently? Did you enjoy the experience?"

"You need to understand, there was no pleasure in the act. I was cold. Hungry. A woman would do anything to satisfy hunger pains. Beg. Steal. Even…"

"What? Tell me."

"Lie with a man. Let him have his way."

"Yes, but was there any pleasure in the moment?"

Madeleine went silent, contemplating the painful memory. "I don't think you understand."

"Explain it to me. I need to understand what to expect when I arrive in New France."

"Marie," Madeleine said, whispering, hoping no one could hear her, "it's a physical act. I hated every moment. A man forcing himself on me, ramming his cock inside of me, and only for the benefit of *his* pleasure. Not mine. I was a vessel to place his cock, nothing more. Not a lady in his eyes."

"So, it hurt?"

"Why do you ask me these questions?"

"Because," she replied, sounding concerned. "I'm an innocent, a virgin, and you have some experience."

Madeleine twisted to face Marie, though she could not see her. "Louise told you the truth. We travel to New France to find a husband. Nothing more. I have no wish to hurt you, but love will not be found in this new world, only commitment, submission, and further loss."

"Why are you so certain of that? Surely there is hope. Good men exist."

"Not in my experience."

"But your father? Surely he was a good example?"

"Hardly," Madeleine huffed, shaking her head. "We won't speak of him."

"Please, don't tell me that…"

"My father made bad decisions in his life, but he was not the one who hurt me most."

"If not your father, what led you to the streets in the first place? Have you no home to return to?"

"I had a home," Madeleine whispered, closing her eyes, remembering her previous life, attempting to quell the rising emotions. "My father took ill. My mother nursed him until he passed away."

"That's terrible. What of your mother?"

"She took ill, too, leaving this world not two weeks after my father."

"Siblings? Do you have any?"

"A brother," Madeleine recalled, rolling her eyes. "Jean Bourbonnais."

"What of him? Why didn't he come to your aid, to support you in your time of need?"

"I don't know. Maybe he's alive; maybe he's dead. He sailed away, a merchant searching for fame and fortune on the high sea. An adventurer, he's never been seen or heard from since. Perhaps he's drowned. I fear he's buried at the bottom of the ocean."

"Your brother could still be alive. A merchant's ambition takes time to prosper."

"It hardly matters now." She yawned, stretching, fighting sleep. "I've lost everything with my parents' death. Coupled with my father's debt and lack of inheritance, I was robbed of my family home, too. Forced to survive on the street. Forced…"

"Tell me what you were going to say."

"I was nothing more than a street rat scouring the rue for scraps. Jean Bourbonnais will never know what happened to his sister, or what I was forced to endure to survive. He'll never find me, if he is alive."

"Madeleine, I'm sorry to learn of your struggles. Maybe something good can come from the king's purpose. Maybe your husband will be kind; maybe he'll care for your child, or if chance finds a way, your brother will find you."

"If he's alive," Madeleine mused, yawning again. "Marie, please go to sleep. Nothing waits for us but the unknown. Leave your worries for another day. It's best we don't concern ourselves with the new world and what lies there until the captain sights land with his spyglass. Only then will we learn the truth of our future."

Marie yawned, rolling to her back. "I prefer to focus on the positive, however, best to sleep and dream. From what you've told me, the reality could be a difficult demon to awaken to."

CHAPTER 4

*J*ulian supervised the officers as they labored, scrutinizing them while they lifted ninety-pound bales of animal pelts, beaver, otter, and bear. He measured their progress, seeing his men wrestling with the weight, carrying the cargo onto the ship and then stowing it inside the hold. He focused on other matters, too, mulling over one small letter he had delivered into the captain's hands. Numb inside, was he feeling *regretful* for this deed? Sighing, he shook his head in defeat, but if he were honest with himself, he had found a sense of relief in the act. If he gave up on the past, he was free to pursue his future.

While he supervised the heavy work of officers moving up and down the gangplank, he remembered the conversation with his commander. Two weeks had passed since his promise had been made, and the time would soon arrive when another ship would reach these shores, carrying his future wife.

Already at sea, the galleon was expected to make land in

late July or early August. He was resigned to one woman's arrival, and he wondered, *who might she be?*

"What ails thee, Julian? Your young face seems marred with wrinkles."

Julian turned to his friend and colleague. A rugged man, Mack sported a full russet beard and his wild hair swept across his shoulders. He seemed comfortable wearing his tanned leather and the smirk on his face helped Julian forget his worries, for now.

"It's nothing. How are you? How is the family?"

"Kiah's given birth to another daughter. Eerin Willow was born early in the spring."

"Another child? That brings your family to… what, nine now?"

"Eight. A son passed over the winter. Kiah still grieves his loss."

"I'm sorry, Mack. Losing a loved one is a difficult burden to bear, and your wife's especially caring. I'm sure she's taking it hard."

"There's a hole in my heart as well," he said with a sigh, staring at the ground. "Perhaps we should discuss other business."

"Of course," Julian replied, regarding Mack meaningfully. "Have you experienced any trade difficulties lately? Earning a living must be difficult with the war troubles in the South?"

"The Iroquois Nation, the Mohawk people, have tried to monopolize the hunting grounds of the Great Lakes. Those insidious bastards," Mack spat on the ground, shaking his head, "they'll be the death of us all. They continue to disrupt the flow of furs for our neighbors to the South, and not without blood being shed."

Julian considered his point, worrying. The Iroquois had threatened their allies, the Wendat and Ottawa natives, to such an extent that trading furs on the northern shores of Lake Ontario was becoming increasingly difficult, forcing explorers to travel further west for their own safety. Still, he worried the fort could be threatened, again, either by the aboriginal people or by the English colonists of New England.

"Do you think we should prepare for an attack? Maybe increase the patrols?"

"Your officers should be on guard; and please mind the forest because a man never knows who's lurking behind the trees, waiting for an opportunity. Especially further south on la Rivière Richelieu. If tensions get much worse, I might bring my family to stay at the fort. It's becoming riskier trading south of la Rivière Saint-Laurent."

"They're more than welcome here. Have you been able to earn a living with the disruption?"

"I'm able to profit in the upper Great Lakes. I have managed to bring a full load of pelts for the return trip of Le Voyager. What of you, Julian? I hear you're taking a bride when the next shipment of women arrives."

Mack had a huge grin on his face. Julian shook his head, still anxious about the situation. "Who told you?"

"News travels fast when it has to do with Julian Benoit."

"Well, I'm good at accepting my orders, and sometimes, I do as I'm told."

"Aye, and maybe you'll enjoy the pleasure that comes with your prize. A man should not be alone."

He had a point. Julian gazed at the ship longingly, wishing he could solve his loneliness by sailing back to France, but he'd given his oath of service. "I should get on that merchant ship and sail back to France. Catherine waits."

"I've never seen a man more loyal than you, but loyalty will not warm your bed at night. I bet you haven't tasted the wares of an aboriginal woman to stem your tide."

"I see the life you share with Kiah, and believe me, Mack, I think it's great you've found the love of your life. I made a commitment to a woman. I have been faithful to that promise."

Mack smacked him on the shoulder. "It appears you're making a new oath."

"I'm breaking a woman's heart."

"You think so? You give Catherine too much power. I bet she's not waiting. She's probably secured a new betrothal while you pine for lips you cannot kiss."

Julian wondered if Mack's estimation might be correct. He had lived in the new world for a year. A long time to be away from the woman he loved. Maybe she had forgotten him. Her communications were less frequent, in fact, he hadn't received a letter from her this spring. Maybe he ached for a love who had forgotten him.

"She would never deceive me," Julian replied, wondering if he was wrong.

"Some advice, my friend?"

"I could tell you to mind your own damn business, but you're not easily dissuaded with your high and mighty opinions."

Mack laughed heartily, pressing closer. "Julian, my good

friend, I can see how much this hurts you, but seek the woman who comes to you, not the one who keeps you waiting."

Mack Chovier nudged Julian on his back, then left his company, progressing toward the ship to secure a space for his hides on the ship's return trip to France. The fur trapper had given Julian a lot to think about. He walked along the shoreline, soon gathering his horse. He urged the iron mare upward, progressing along the hill, climbing, retreating to the fort.

Why had he revealed such personal information? His letter of regret had already been passed into the captain's hands. The decision was made. The note would soon be enroute to France. There was no turning back now.

CHAPTER 5

*M*adeleine tried to mark the passing days, but time ceased to hold meaning. Life onboard ship held an air of simplicity, and someone was always on hand to take care of her. The meals were good in the beginning, but now as animal stock and supplies lessened, hardtack became a horrible foodstuff that dried out her mouth and lay heavy in her stomach, and the only water left onboard tasted stale.

The close quarters didn't help. Below deck, human sweat fouled the air and all too often someone was upset with somebody else.

She found herself spending most of her time on the quarterdeck. Gazing at the ocean, she constantly reflected on the port she had left behind, and the port ahead that bound her future to an unknown man. Monotony. Night and day stretched into light and dark, and she was constantly aware of the damp cold with only the sea and the company of other women or crew members to amuse her. Cold, she shivered constantly. She became frail.

Often, she'd sit in the company of Marie, silent, her spirit defeated, having nothing more to say. She would lie on the quarterdeck, wrapped in a blanket, staring at cerulean-blue skies and clouds puffed white, hoping yet another bout of seasickness might pass.

Would this voyage ever be over? *And this too, shall pass. Hopefully, not with her own death.*

"Girls—" Geneviève exclaimed, her tone brimming with excitement. "Come, come quick. A sea monster…"

Madeleine rolled to her knees and rose to a standing position. Weak, she wobbled forward, clutching her blanket to her neck. She leaned against the wooden railing. "Where?" she asked, staring at bluish-gray waters. Two spouts of spray spurted from the sea, not fifty yards out.

"There!" Geneviève yelled, pointing, jumping. "Did you see it?"

"What is that?" Marie yelled.

Several other girls rushed over, some quicker than others, everyone searching the sea for life. "Look!" Geneviève shouted, pointing over the railing. "Just there…"

As they watched, a black creature emerged from the deep, breaching the surface and jumping high into the air. Just as quickly, it plunged into the sea, leaving a huge white splash in its wake.

"Ooh, a whale…"

Geneviève jumped, young and full of excitement. Still more girls rushed to the railing. "Did you see it?"

Madeleine smiled slightly, seeing the joy in the young

woman's face. She had obviously developed sea legs. "Quite large," she remarked, swaying on her feet. "If I wasn't so tired, I'd think it amazing."

Closer to the ship, a second creature breached the water. It was larger than the first and she watched in amazement as the mammal burst through the blue ocean, soared momentarily and then returned to the water, splashing a tidal wave, and disappearing underneath.

Geneviève clapped her hands, her laughter floating on the wind. Louise stepped away from the railing, breathing rapidly.

"Are you afraid?" Madeleine asked.

"Certainly not."

"There's no shame if you are. The mammal came close to us, and it's big besides."

Her face expressed her annoyance. She sashayed toward Madeleine, wearing a venomous guise. "Don't attempt to forge a friendship now, Madame. You and I shall never be friends."

"Another," Geneviève squealed, dancing on the deck.

"And there, too." Marie squealed, relaxed, watching as a spurt of water took to the air.

"I suppose not, if you continue to call me names…" Madeleine said to Louise, her head dizzy. She began to sway; a strong buzzing began between her ears.

"Madame, does a demon possess you? What is wrong with you?"

Madeleine collapsed on the deck, everything went black.

❧

UNCONSCIOUS, Madeleine twisted on the gurney, wrinkling her face, smelling a noxious substance pressed close to her nose. A hand patted her face, and the perpetrator's voice sounded serious.

"Wake up, Madeleine, come on now, open your eyes."

A familiar voice called from a distance, a place she could not reach. "Papa?" she mumbled, trying to open her eyes, but she was so tired.

"I'm not your father. Come on, young lady, wake up."

Opening her eyes, Madeleine established eye contact with surgeon Martin and a concerned Marie. She lay inside a box-like hammock in the sick bay cabin. "What happened? Where am I?"

Standing over her, a man with red hair, sea-blue eyes and a full beard looked at her, his expression full of concern. "You've had a fall. You're in the sick bay."

"Sick bay?"

"I want to assure you, you're safe. I've done an initial examination and have discovered a condition. Mademoiselle Chauvet, perhaps you should leave us as what I need to discuss with my patient, must be said in private."

"I don't want my friend to leave. I give you permission to speak freely. What condition have you discovered?"

"I'm not comfortable discussing the matter with your friend present. Our discussion is of a confidential nature."

Madeleine stared at him, concluding his diagnosis might have serious implications for her future. She suspected she already knew what he would say. Swallowing, she hoped she would not be sick again, but lying inside the sick bay hammock, she didn't feel the ocean's sway as much. "I trust Marie. Please, Doctor Martin, get on with it."

"All right," he said with a grimace, glancing at Marie momentarily, "do you know you're with child?"

Madeleine closed her eyes shut tight. She shook her head not wanting to admit the truth, but the truth had been discovered. "How did you find out?"

"I'm a doctor. You've been sick for days. When you collapsed, the crew carried you to my quarters. I examined you. While your clothing hides your condition, you're starting to show."

She nodded, sensing the admonishment in his eyes. Marie grasped her hand and squeezed her fingers. "I can imagine what you're thinking. Please let me assure you, I'm not a prostitute."

"I have not accused you of impropriety, but young woman, you're bound for the colony and given your present condition, you're not fit to take a husband. I must advise the captain of your condition and the nuns on shore too, when you arrive at Ville de Québec."

Ashamed, Madeleine glanced away.

"Why?" Marie declared, staring the doctor in the face. "What gives you the authority to destroy my friend's hope of a better future? She has as much right to a husband as the other women onboard this ship with, with childless wombs."

"Mademoiselle Chauvet, you must understand, it's not right to burden a husband with another man's child."

Madeleine nodded in agreement, but Marie persisted with her argument. "The king wants to grow the colony, so this child is important to the future of New France. What does it matter which man supplied the seed? Miss Bourbonnais' baby needs a father. You cannot say anything that will risk the child's, or the mother's future."

Tears pooled in Madeleine's eyes. "If you reveal my secret, you condemn us once more to poverty."

"I understand your plight," he said, reclining in a wooden chair. "I care about the situation, the unborn child, however…"

"If you speak to the captain," Marie protested, "you'll ruin this child's chance of a better life. The baby will be an orphan condemned. Be a man. Pretend you never discovered Madeleine's condition."

He shook his head. "I cannot. I'm a surgeon on board a ship, bound by a code of ethics. I want to help, I really do."

"Then help!" Marie pleaded, taking his hand. "Save this woman's future."

"Dear me," he said in exasperation, shaking his head and running his fingers through unruly red hair, but the semblance of a smile gave both women hope. They waited expectantly for him to reply.

"Why do I always fall prey to the advances of women?"

"You'll keep my secret?"

He patted her hand. "Mais oui, Mademoiselle Madeleine, but only on one condition."

"Yes?" they said hopefully and at the same time.

"You will tell your suitor the truth, and let him decide, prior to the marriage contract."

"She will not!" Marie gulped, rising from her chair. "You're a doctor, not a magistrate. You fix hearts, not break them! You're risking being thrown overboard, fish bait for the whales. And there's some twenty women onboard who can assist me!"

"Mademoiselle Marie, I fear for the husband who chooses you for a wife. You have a wicked heart."

"If only I could marry her myself," Madeleine quipped, taking a deep breath. "Such a supportive friend would make a good husband."

"Enough talk, ladies, you rule a hard bargain. We'll have no more talk of this, this condition. I will keep your secret and let God be the judge. As you say, I'm a doctor."

"Thank you, Doc Martin."

"As for the patient's care, as you are settled in the sick bay, it's my advice that you sleep here tonight. Your friend may join you as there is a spare hammock."

"Finally, you see reason," Marie replied, climbing into the spare hammock.

"For the rest of the journey, I will watch over you to ensure mother and child are cared for. However, once you leave the ship, your future is up to you."

Madeleine sighed, grateful to Marie for being her champion. "Thank you again, Doc Martin."

CHAPTER 6

LATE JULY 1666

*M*adeleine lay on the quarterdeck suffering from bouts of dizziness as the galleon cut through the ocean, sailing closer to New France. Though a pleasant wind blew warm against her cheeks, fatigue gripped her. She didn't have the strength to lift her limbs or move her fingers. After weeks at sea, she was accustomed to the boat creaking, and had become comfortable with the groaning. She knew the ship would not break apart.

"Madeleine?"

Someone was calling her name. A hand patted her cheek.

"Come now, young woman. Don't do this to me, wake up."

"No."

"Water. Get me some water."

Madeleine did not want to drink the stale liquid; she'd

only vomit again. A sound buzzed between her ears, her head hurt, though her stomach had finally settled. And she was tired. "Let me rest."

"I think not, young woman." The doctor became more insistent and placed smelling salts to her nose. She scrunched her face.

"Good girl," he said, raising her head. "Now take a drink. You've been lying in the sun too long, without water, without food, and you're too hot."

A spout of water nudged against her lips, squirted inside her mouth. "Awful," she said with a grimace, obeying, swallowing.

"Doesn't matter what it tastes like. You need to keep hydrated. Come on, take one more sip."

She opened her eyes, but the light was so bright it hurt to look at it, so she closed them again.

"No, Maddie. Listen to the doc. Wake up. Drink."

"Sabine..." Madeleine murmured, opening her eyes again, searching for Marie. "She's stopped coughing. Is she better?"

Marie's expression soured. She glanced away.

"Doc Martin?"

"I assure you, Sabine is free of pain."

Madeleine nibbled at her lower lip, worrying. "She's not better? Will you tell me the truth? I'll find out when she's not in her bunk tonight."

"No one will hide the awful truth from you. Sadly, Sabine passed during the night."

"Oh," Madeleine said, closing her eyes, willing herself not

to cry, though she had barely known the woman. "A watery grave?"

"We will not speak of it."

Madeleine saw how the death affected the surgeon. Gray dimmed the sensitive tissues beneath his sea-blue eyes. Perhaps fatigue compelled him to close his eyes, in defeat. She had never seen him at a loss for words.

"Land ahoy!" An overseer yelled. A cheer erupted from the women and crew members alike and Madeleine was glad of the distraction.

"Land?" she said, opening her eyes again, her hand at her forehead to shield her eyes from the light. "Help me to my feet, Marie. I want to see it."

Doc Martin and Marie took hold of her hands and assisted her to rise. "What's wrong, Marie? You seem worried."

"I was." She took a deep quivering breath. "About you."

Madeleine swayed on her feet, stepping tentatively toward the railing. "I'm standing. With God's grace, I will be well. Come now. Let us see this land."

They walked to the handrail. At first, the New World was no more than a spot on the horizon, the landmass so small it didn't appear like anything at all. But as the ship sailed closer, massive cliff edges emerged. Their stone-laden sides brown like sand and in places carved by the wind, they stretched upward into the sky, with the tops covered with green-needled trees.

Captain François stood on the quarterdeck, too. A spyglass held in his hand. "What land is in sight?" she asked.

"The Grand Banks of Newfoundland," he said with a grin. "And the best fish stocks you'll ever taste."

"When will we make land?"

"Get some rest. We have many leagues yet to travel. We won't make port at Ville de Québec for at least two more weeks."

"Why do you smile when we have far to go?"

"Ah, Madeleine, I understand more than most how weeks at sea can bend the human mind. The waiting, the most difficult burden to bear."

"Too far, to ever consider returning to my homeland."

"There isn't a man or woman on board this ship who hasn't yearned for solid ground beneath their feet," he offered, patting her shoulder. "The journey's been long. Difficult. We were blown off course twice in my estimation, and there were moments when I thought…"

"What did you think?"

"Well, that the ship might be lost," he said with a grimace, but then a smile brightened his expression. "But the end of this voyage is in sight now."

"Thank God."

"You do not look at all well, Madeleine. Perhaps you should take yourself to the sick bay."

"I was going to suggest the same," Doc Martin said.

Madeleine accepted the surgeon's arm and followed him as he escorted her to his quarters.

"Make anchor," the captain yelled. "Tonight, we feast on the best fish stocks. Welcome to the New World, ladies. Mayhap tonight, we'll take a longboat to shore, and give everyone a rest from the rocking before we set sail again in the morning."

"Two weeks," Madeleine said with a sigh, "seems like an eternity."

"All things must pass. Before you know it, we will make land in Ville de Québec."

CHAPTER 7

The ship was sighted upriver in the early morning hours of August 11, 1666. When a fellow officer notified Julian of the boat's imminent arrival, he dressed quickly, eager to get to the dock. But once he stood on the wood-planked wharf, doubt filled his heart. The galleon sailed closer and he watched her come, the boat carrying his future wife.

The sun hung low on the eastern horizon, but as the golden rays lit the water, sparkling diamonds danced across the wide band of water. It created a peaceful effect, his heart should have been gladdened by the ship's sighting, but his forehead furrowed with worry as it sailed closer.

If not for Catherine, my heart would be glad.

The arrival of *les filles du Roi*, the King's daughters, was nigh. Fresh fruit for his men, and for him as well, if he so desired to partake.

The ship edged closer to the shore and Julian watched the crew preparing the lines. The sailors soon threw a length of cord to able-bodied seamen waiting on the dock to assist with the mooring. Many women stood on the decks. He tried to scrutinize each pretty face, whether blonde, brunette or redhead, and nearly every girl wore a bonnet.

Which lady, he wondered, would be his wife?

The tall brunette with the gray woolen blanket wrapped around her shoulders? The lady wearing the mulberry dress, or the several petite damsels who shouted from the quarterdeck, waving their hands vigorously, perhaps excited to leave the boat for the men waiting on the shore.

The men who had gathered were just as eager, and they waved back in response. He understood their excitement. There simply were not enough marriageable women to choose from in this native land; this was the only way for most men to have a wife. It would not be long now.

"Good morning," René said, coming to stand beside him. "I see our journey is soon to begin."

Julian gazed at his commander and the women on deck, his arms folded across his chest in resignation. René's officer's clothing was well presented. Not so much as a speck of dust on his long-coat, or a wrinkle on his white shirt. He must have had it freshly starched. Maybe he really wanted a wife.

"I didn't think you'd come. I didn't believe you'd taken a serious interest in a wife."

"Why would you question my sincerity? Did you think I was jesting?" he laughed, slapping Julian on the shoulder. "Surely you understand that my word is my bond, solid like the ground we stand on."

"I've always understood your swagger."

"Do not irritate me. I've been looking forward to this

moment. I'm glad we engaged in conversation, bringing us to this occasion. I'm titillated by the possibilities. What of you?"

"I'd rather not say."

"Still sore on the subject? Feel like you're standing on quicksand? My good man," René chuckled, "get a grip; show some enthusiasm for the women about to make land. Tread carefully, too, for if you choose my pretty penny, it's a duel at dawn for us, Monsieur."

"You wound me, René."

Distracted, Julian observed Sister Abby, the church directress, and three sisters of the faith. Accompanied by Bishop François de Laval and Intendant Jean Talon, the assemblage promenaded to the ship. *An audience to welcome the King's Daughters.* Julian and René bowed their heads in respect, waiting for the gangway to be lowered. A trumpeter sounded a horn and soon after the first girls left the boat.

Julian watched Jean Talon shake each girl's hand, welcoming the women to the shores of Ville de Québec, Canada. Smiling, the Intendant took an avid interest and engaged each girl in conversation, but this was his ambition to bring the women to New France. He should be excited by the outcome. Julian was yet undecided.

The women ambled along the boardwalk, coming closer to him. Nervous, he prepared to welcome them. He swallowed, scrutinizing each pretty face. Some women returned his gesture, others expressed melancholy.

He grinned like a young schoolboy as he accepted the brief touch of the first girl's fingers on his palm. "A good day to you, Monsieur," she said with a slim smile, curtsying.

"And to you," Julian replied.

He mouthed similar responses to each woman while scrutinizing the parade of possibilities, studying the various expressions, and the avid interest on each pretty face. But beauty did not concern him overly. A man wanted specific traits in his wife. A kind soul. A hard worker. A woman he could take home to his mother. How could a man choose a bride, an exceptional woman, from a chance meeting?

An older woman approached him where he stood. She wore a bemused expression on her face, lavender curls escaped her coif. Wide hips. He wondered if she had already borne children. A widow, perhaps?

"Captain?" she asked.

The impertinence bothered him. "Oui, Mademoiselle," he replied, bowing to her in a show of respect. "Welcome to Ville de Québec."

"A long journey, I'm grateful to have finally stepped off the boat."

"And we're delighted to make your acquaintance." René beamed with joy, interrupting. Julian looked suspiciously at his friend as the commander took hold of her hand, his cheeks flushing with pleasure. Really? Julian was surprised.

"And what is your name, good lady?" René asked.

"Mademoiselle Louise," she muttered, curtseying, her cheeks matching the same crimson color as the commander's. "A good day to you, Monsieur. Monsieur?"

"You may call me René, if you don't mind dismissing the formality."

Surprised at his commander's joviality, Julian glanced away. A petite woman wearing a mulberry dress ambled close. She was swathed in a gray woolen blanket. He scrutinized her pallid, colorless expression. Underneath her bonnet, her chestnut hair fell in messy curls to her waist. She was a captivating beauty. He was attracted to her amber eyes and porcelain skin.

He extended his hand and she tentatively put her fingers on his palm. He didn't expect it. A jolt of emotion squeezed his heart. "Mademoiselle…"

"I'm sorry, Monsieur. I'm not well."

"It's a frightful journey, long and difficult." He could not think, what should he say? "What is your name?"

"Madeleine—" She curtsied, swaying, squeezing his fingers firmly but more to keep her balance. "Madeleine Bourbonnais."

"Monsieur," she begged, her voice strained; she stepped closer, clinging to his hand. Her expression seemed panicked. "I'm going to…"

She collapsed, falling into his arms.

Julian pulled her close, bringing her to his chest, taking her to the ground. "She's fainted," he cried out, "help!"

In that moment, Julian forgot Catherine. He had caught an angel in his arms and now that he held the softness of her feminine form, he didn't know what to do.

CHAPTER 8

 adeleine opened her eyes. Confused, she lay on a hard-wooden surface, smelling the scent of sulfur. Surgeon Martin must have administered the noxious substance, again.

"Where am I?" She grumbled, staring at the doctor, but also perusing the many people who gathered nearby.

"The land of opportunity, Mademoiselle Madeleine, Ville de Québec, New France."

"What happened to me? I was…"

"Ah, your fragile sensibilities. You fainted again."

"Mademoiselle," a masculine voice intruded, "you collapsed in my arms."

Madeleine turned to the sound, seeing the man she had met before. She searched his expression, perusing the gold flecks in his hazel eyes, remembering the brief touch of his hand. He knelt beside her.

"Thank you for your kindness, Monsieur."

"Ahem," Surgeon Martin said, kneeling on her other side,

"pleasantries aside, 'tis best I assist you to the boarding house; you will require rest after your spell. Take my hand. I'll escort you there myself."

"If you'd permit me, Doctor, I'd like to offer my care, and escort this young woman myself."

"My charge requires the attention of someone who is medically trained. She's weak, and it's been a difficult journey. It's best I offer the care."

Madeleine disregarded the doctor to scrutinize the mysterious gentleman. Was he an officer? His uniform and controlled mannerism seemed to acknowledge his profession. He knelt closer and she felt her cheeks flame with recognition of his masculinity.

"Is that what you require?" he asked, staring. "I'm not medically trained, but anyone can see your time spent at sea has been hard on you. Permit me to escort you to your residence. Mademoiselle, I'm not ready to leave your company."

Smiling, he held out his hand. Glimpsing a genuine interest in his hazel eyes, Madeleine should have been excited for his regard, as she required a man's notice and needed his consideration, but she viewed him like other males, another man who wanted more than she could give. *What might he want? Something of a physical nature?* Regardless that she wanted, *no needed*, a solid foundation from a man like him, too.

"Kind of you," she said with a grimace, "to offer your care, but as the surgeon says, I'm in need of medical attention. Perhaps another time."

"Mademoiselle, once you're safely established at the

boarding house, may I call on you?"

She hadn't expected a man to take an interest so soon, but in her present condition, the sooner she championed a man's attention, the better. She perused his expression, mused that his demeanor seemed grim. Why had he posed the question?

"You may call on me at your convenience."

"I bid you adieu, and wish you a speedy recovery."

"Merci, Monsieur."

He retreated, and she watched him take his leave. A virile masculine man, he was well shaped from the top of his broad shoulders to the thickness of muscular thighs that supported long legs, tucked into black leather boots that clicked on the wood planking as he walked. Yes, he was a handsome man. She would have to engage in her best behavior if she was to capture his heart.

CHAPTER 9

The morning after the daughters' arrival in New France, the girls who had chosen to remain in Ville de Québec were ushered inside the boarding house's parlor. Madeleine still felt weak, but fluids and healthy food had helped to restore her health somewhat. A firm ground that didn't sway like the sea helped, too.

A sister nun stood at the front of the room. She was gowned in black and her facial features expressed a strict self-confidence. Madeleine waited, afraid to hear her speech.

"While living in this house," she said sternly, pacing near the assembled women, "you have much to learn. You have come to New France, a place of hardship. In many ways, a bleak world much different from the homeland you sailed away from."

She stopped talking, seeming to scrutinize each woman's face as if to satisfy her point.

"Your purpose is to meet a husband and assist with the colonization. This is why the king favored you with a dowry to take the hand of a husband. To this end, men will come to call on you. Introductions will take place in this room and as a group. No woman," she said with some emphasis, "is to entertain a gentleman alone, nor leave this house and set out alone with a…"

"Might I ask a question?" Marie asked, raising her hand.

"You may."

"Will we have a say in our choice of husband?"

"Good question. You're not cattle. No man will visit this place expecting to purchase a cow. I expect the officers, or other types of laborers, to act as gentlemen."

"How will the meetings be organized?" Louise asked, not bothering to ask for permission.

"Some officers have made their requests. Times are being managed."

"And the meetings," Geneviève hinted, nibbling at her lip. "What can we expect?"

"They'll take place in the parlor, a perfect setting for introductions and cordial conversation. You'll want to ask questions, of course."

Marie leaned close to Geneviève. "Little good that will do. Some men are born to lie."

"What did you say?" the nun asked, stepping toward them. "Please share with the group."

"I was saying, what if the men tell tales? What if they lie?"

"I assure you," the sister replied, stepping closer to Marie. "The men of New France have no reason to lie. Most officers have sworn their duty to the new world, our sovereign God, and of course, the king."

"Of course, Sister Abby. I meant no disrespect."

"Mesdemoiselles, you shall not worry about a man's intentions. They are obvious. Most men want companionship. A support only realized with a wife. And you'll be chaperoned, never left alone with your suitor. If you're uncomfortable for any reason, you may end the meeting."

"What if we're happy with the suitor?"

"If the first meeting goes favorably, choose to see him again."

Madeleine looked at Marie, who tapped her on the knee. "Maybe the officer will come to court you."

"We are getting ahead of ourselves, but when a gentleman chooses a lady, and she accepts his proposal, a marriage contract will be drawn up. After an acceptable period, which is agreeable to both parties, you will be married. But you must be prepared for the life you will live. We need to ensure you can take care of your household."

"What will we need to learn, Sister Abby?" Geneviève asked, her face full of curiosity.

"Another good question. Life is difficult in New France. You will be taught the simplest means of caring for your husband's household. Maintaining a proper home requires cleanliness, cooking a meal, stitchery, perhaps raising and feeding livestock, seeding and growing crops."

Marie giggled. "Mistress Louise, I bet you've never handled a needle and thread in your entire life."

"You might be surprised at my skills, Mistress Marie, you sassy sow. I'm an expert at embroidery."

"An expert at embroidery? How delightful."

"Now, now," Sister Abby said, "I will not tolerate name calling. In this house, we are all daughters of New France. Of chance and opportunity. I can see some of you come from different social classes. Ladies, there is only one class in this country and her name is work. To survive, you'll need to support each other. Friends fare better than enemies."

Marie pouted. Louise soured. Madeleine contemplated.

"Kindness is important, ladies. When the cold winds of winter howl, you'll seek each other in friendship, if only to keep each other warm. I promise you that."

"We'll see about that," Louise said.

"Something we can agree on." Marie replied.

Madeleine wasn't sure what to think. She didn't want Louise's friendship, but neither did she want the woman as an enemy.

"When will the first visit happen?" Madeleine asked, feeling a fluttering sensation in her stomach. "An officer has asked to call on me."

"Captain Julian Benoit will call on you tonight, young woman."

"Tonight?" Madeleine contemplated seeing him again, her face blushing pink. The man whose arms she had fallen into, who perhaps she had come across the ocean to meet, would visit her tonight? She wondered about him already.

CHAPTER 10

The sun had set, and the time had arrived for Madeleine to meet Captain Benoit. Inside her bedchamber she shared with Marie, she stood in front of a rectangular looking glass, brushing long layers of chestnut hair. She could see she had lost a lot of weight during her voyage across the Atlantic. Gray hollows dimmed her amber eyes, and although her skin had gained a bronzed glow, her eyes seemed sunken and less bright.

She brushed her hair until the silken strands shone, perusing her appearance, twisting back and forth to ensure her dress was prim and proper. She was ready to meet the captain and this time she'd not embarrass herself by fainting.

"Will he like me?" she wondered aloud, gazing at her reflection in the mirror.

"How could he not?" Marie replied, coming to stand beside her. "You're a beauty, Maddie. If he's not smitten by your pithy glow, he'll take one look at your big brown eyes and fall impossibly in love."

Madeleine glanced downward, twisting a lock of hair between her fingers. She appreciated her friend didn't think less of her because she was with child, but she still felt guilty for holding this secret, all the same.

"But he's handsome. He could choose from any of the king's wards; a girl less frail with higher cheekbones, merrier eyes, a slimmer waist," she said with a grimace, wincing. "Why do you think he wants to have a meeting with me?"

"Perhaps you should mind the reflection in the mirror, my friend, or ask the man yourself," Marie replied, pinching her cheeks, causing her face to blush pink. "Make a good impression," she said with a wink. "Mind your manners, choose your words carefully, and snatch him up fast or I'll steal him for myself."

"You wouldn't dare."

Marie chuckled, stepping away. "I could. I'm in need of a husband as well, and love has brought me far across the sea for such a man."

Madeleine giggled, grasping her friend's hand. "You don't mean it. But of course, an officer might catch your notice. Did you see anyone who fancied your attention after our arrival?"

"I've caught the attention of one or two men. I don't mind telling you, I winked, twirled my skirt, licked my lips, even offered a glimpse of my ankle. My mother taught me how to make an impression."

"You're scandalous, Marie. You carry the manners of a lady and the heart of a true vixen."

"Isn't that what every man desires? A *lady* when in the

company of a gentleman and a *sexy siren* at the day's end? A weight perfectly balanced?"

"You're naughty." Madeleine giggled, pressing closer. "You make me laugh and I need the humor, but if you've seen someone, you must share your secret."

"Everything in time," Marie said, grinning, turning away as the sister entered their small room. "I will not alarm my fragile heart with false hope."

"Mademoiselle Bourbonnais," Sister Abby entreated, "Captain Benoit's here to make your acquaintance."

"I best not keep him waiting."

She flashed Marie a brilliant smile and followed Sister Abby from the room, soon descending a ladder to the lower floor. She walked along a short corridor to the front parlor where the captain waited. When she entered the chamber, his back was to her, but when he turned, holding his hat in his hands, she sighed.

Dressed in the French uniform of a Carignan-Salières Regimental officer, he made a handsome impression. Madeleine drew in a quick breath, pausing to study his stature. He was tall and straight of back and his brown long-coat fit his broad chest well and tapered neatly to his waist. His matching breeches and snug hose hugged his legs admirably well, too.

A handsome brute, Madeleine mused silently. She could not seem to stop pondering his hazel eyes, and he didn't shy away from the scrutiny.

"Captain Benoit, permit me to introduce Madeleine Bourbonnais."

She curtsied, as Sister Constance at the Hôpital de

Salpêtrière had taught her to do. She remembered the stern lecture: '*always present yourself as a lady, prostitutes suffer a quick coupling; ladies stand the test of time. Make no mistake, Mademoiselle, you are a lady!*'

Trying to hold to her convictions, she stepped forward, curtsying, soon accepting his outstretched hand.

"Enchanté, Mademoiselle," he said, not breaking eye contact. "I'm delighted to make your acquaintance."

He held her fingers, refusing to release her appendages. She permitted his grasp to linger, gazing into the depths of interest within his eyes, wondering what he saw as he looked at her. "Thank you, Captain. A pleasure to meet you, too."

"Please take a seat," Sister Abby insisted, motioning to a rectangular oak table set with white linens and a porcelain tea service. "The cook has made tea. I will have it brought in shortly. I trust I can leave you alone to see to the work in the kitchen?"

"Of course," the captain replied, seeming irritated by the comment. "I'm a gentleman. I'll act accordingly."

Still, he did not release her hand. "If you'll permit me," he offered, leading her to a rush-seated chair. He pulled it out, assisted her to sit, and only then released his grip. A gentleman as he had said, Madeleine mused to herself.

He sat in the high-back chair opposite her. "Tell me about yourself," he requested, coming straight to the point. "Where did you reside in France?"

"Paris." It was a one-word answer. She didn't elaborate further. Maybe she was captured by the intensity of his stare. Maybe she didn't know what more to say. The room seemed too small; she tried to breathe. Butterflies were dancing in her stomach. *Butterflies?*

"And what of your family, are they from Paris as well?"

"They're dead."

"Is this why you've journeyed to New France? Because your family is gone and you seek a new hope, a new chance at life?"

"Yes," she whispered, as the feeling came again. Was the baby stirring?

"Madeleine, do you find me disagreeable?"

"Not at all, Captain Benoit."

"Why the disquiet, the one-word answers?"

Uncomfortable, she gazed at the intensity of his inquiry, her hands placed primly on her lap. She studied his smooth angular face, the strong jawline and full lips that would in time demand their payment. She considered her past and knew if he chose her, she'd have to touch his lips. *Did she want to?* Sister Constance had confided: '*finding a husband is your only option for a good life. You will have to accept your duties—as his wife.*'

But did she want a husband? Was he the one? Could she deceive him; he seemed so kind?

"Would you believe me, Monsieur, if I told you I was shy?"

He leaned closer, clasped his hands, and placed both elbows on the table. "Your eyes. A hidden truth tells me you're not a shy woman. If I were a betting man?"

"What would you gamble?" She glanced downward, leaning away from his scrutiny.

"You have a story to tell. I would like to hear it."

Indeed. She had many stories she could confide, but he would not like them. Men such as him had betrayed her, used her for their own selfish needs. Had gone so far as to seed a child within her womb. Shyly, she glanced his way. "It's best not to share certain stories."

"Why?"

"Not you as well, Monsieur, subjecting a lady to a single word as a response? What could that mean?"

They ceased their conversation when the sister nun returned with the teapot. The steam rose above their cups as she poured. After, she placed the pot in the middle of the table, retreating to a corner of the room to chaperone their discussion.

"What of you, Captain Benoit? What qualities do you require in a wife? This is why you're here with me? To find a wife?"

"A wife." The word seemed to upset him. His face crinkled. He gazed away. "I want my wife to be like... well?"

"Someone you used to know? A woman who shares the qualities of someone you admire, perhaps a motherly figure?"

A slight smile curved his lips. "My mama would be delighted if her son found a proper wife. You see, Mademoiselle, she yearns for grandchildren. My papa, he thinks of children who might take his family name. So, he's more insistent on a commitment."

Madeleine reached for the teacup and saucer. *A proper woman?* She could certainly provide him with a child, but not one who would carry his name, at least not the first.

"You frown again?"

"The discussion of children saddens me, Captain. A gift I can never give my parents."

"What happened to your parents?"

Taking a sip of tea, Madeleine remembered her father and mother. Good and kind people, *at least in life*, their title and good names had died with them. "They perished of an illness, a wasting disease."

"I'm sorry. What of your siblings? Do you have any?"

"A brother Jean, but I've not seen him in years. A merchant, he may have perished at sea."

"He could be alive?"

"If he is alive," Madeleine retorted, gritting her teeth. "He will be dead if he ever returns home."

"You intrigue me now. You must tell me why your brother should suffer an ill fate."

"You will not think the worse of me for the telling?"

He reached across the table and grasped her fingers. She didn't pull away, bearing his touch. "You must tell me. Let me decide for myself."

Madeleine pulled away from his touch, took another sip of tea, swallowed, then placed the cup and saucer on the table. "My father, Louis Bourbonnais, was a gambler," she stated, angering simply from uttering his name. "When he and then my mother passed away, the creditors came calling. They seized our assets, the furniture, the home, even my fine clothing. I was thrown into the street wearing my day dress and a cloak. I stole a piece of my mother's jewelry. I was subjected to…"

"You poor dear, how did you survive such an ordeal?"

"Will you think less of me for the telling?"

"That depends on what you admit."

"I lived off the street," Madeleine began, gazing downward in shame, her hands clasped against her lap, unable to meet his expression. "I searched for my food like a street rat, begging sometimes, stealing too, until such time I was forced into a home of sorts at the Hôpital Général."

"You poor dear. How dreadful."

"Do you think the less of me?" She gazed at him warily.

"Should I? Is there something more I should ask of you?"

"Captain, I want to assure you that until the passing of my parents, I came from a prosperous upper-class family. I was a lady."

He stretched forward. "Mademoiselle, you're still a lady. An unfortunate chain of events cannot alter your true nature."

Madeleine endured his scrutiny, hesitantly looking across the fine table. She didn't deserve his attention. She was stained. "Not every man would think so."

"I must press you on that point. What do you know of other men?"

She grimaced, swallowing, searching for a wise retort. "They can be less than kind when the occasion suits them."

"I'll never be unkind."

"You have a code of honor?"

"I'm an officer, Madeleine. Honor is a matter of pride and commitment, but I do confess that I'm not perfect. No man was made perfect. Do you think I could call on you again?"

He stared at her with an intensity that frightened her. She understood the look and the expected consequence. She saw the need in his hazel eyes. *The hunger.* Madeleine understood that degree of wanting. It led to *touching…* She didn't want to receive passion *in that way*, by any man, ever again.

'You'll have to submit to your husband…'

Could she satisfy the needs of a husband? The emotional, the physical? She wasn't completely comfortable with the prospect of an intimate relationship. Could not imagine a man touching her, *like that*, ever again, but she peered directly into his eyes—*smiling slimly*—doing only what was necessary to survive.

"Yes," she replied, lying straight to his face, feeling a movement in her belly, once more. "I'd like to make your acquaintance again, Captain Benoit."

"It would be my pleasure if you'd call me by my first name. Julian."

"Julian—"

"Tomorrow afternoon, or is that too soon?"

"I shall look forward to it."

Taking a final sip of his tea, he rose from his chair. Madeleine stood, too. She saw Captain Julian would have kissed her hand, but Sister Abby gave him a stern regard. They said their awkward goodbyes and he left her company.

Madeleine stood at the doorway and watched him retreat into the night. Breathing softly, she held her hand atop her belly, remembering how it had felt when he had touched her. And she reluctantly admitted, his warmth had felt good.

The baby stirred again.

"Tell me, what were your first impressions of Captain Benoit?" Marie asked when Madeleine returned to their room.

She leaned against their door. "He wants to see me again. I think that's a good outcome."

"He does? When?"

"Tomorrow."

"Maddie, this is a good outcome. The captain must be interested in you and as I understand, these pairings can move fast."

"I suppose so," Madeleine said with a sigh, walking to a small bed. She sat and removed her bonnet from her head, freeing her hair.

"What is it?" Marie asked, sitting on the bed across from Madeleine. "When everything you want is within reach, why do you seem so glum?"

Madeleine held her head in her hands. The weight of the world pressed in, causing her mind to ache. "I'm deceiving him. The dishonesty doesn't sit right with me. He's a good man, Marie. A woman can tell."

"Be happy, he is. Maybe he'll be kind to you when he learns the truth."

"He'll find out," Madeleine gasped, trying to regain her composure, "and when he does, what then? He'll hate me."

"I can't help you with this uncertainty. You could tell him you're with child, but then you would have to face the consequences. Have you considered what the after-effects might be?"

Madeleine thought about Marie's statement. She'd lose the chance of a father for her child, a future for herself, and perhaps be sent back to France to face ridicule and shame. She couldn't take the risk. She was caught in a trap of her own making.

"There's something else."

"Yes?"

She reached forward and grabbed Marie's hand. "I felt the baby move for the first time."

"You did?" Marie's expression changed to one of wonder. "Now, you appear as if you might cry. Tears of happiness, or sorrow?"

"Marie?" Madeleine took a breath for courage. "I'll be a mother soon. I wish I wasn't with child. If the fates had been kind, I'd have lost the baby. Not having the child would solve the problem."

"Ill wishes can deliver bad omens. They should never be spoken aloud." Marie chastised her, patting her hand. "Children are a blessing, no matter how they've come to be. No one can divine the future, but I will pray for you, Maddie, that your future and the days ahead will find a positive resolution."

CHAPTER 11

When Julian had retired to his bedchamber the night before, succumbing to sleep had been a horrible struggle. Conflicted, he had punched his pillow, his hapless mind unable to resolve the anxiety triggered by a woman named *Madeleine*.

Giving up on his rest, he left his quarters to watch the sunrise, standing beside la Rivière Saint-Laurent. It was commitment day. If he were to submit to his commander's orders, a decision must be made. *Today.* To accept or not to accept a woman from across the ocean.

The pressure to take her hand in marriage had its implications, yet he focused on his first impressions. She was beautiful and any fool would find her desirable. He sucked in his breath, marveling at her loveliness, wanting for… companionship, perhaps a sampling of the physical. *Oh yes, physical.* But her assertions had caused him to question. When had he finally fallen asleep, to dream, to recognize his own truth?

He was lonely and longing for feminine companionship.

But something was wrong. He tried to remember their conversation from the previous day. *What had she hidden from him? What had been left unsaid?* What statement had Madeleine disclosed that had bothered him?

He left the riverside and walked to his commander's lodgings. Soon after entering, he removed his slouch hat and held it in his hands. René looked up from his work and pondered Julian with an avid interest.

"You're upset. What's wrong, Julian?"

"I have come to a decision," Julian said, swallowing. "I have chosen the woman I will propose to."

"Fantastic news. Why then do you look like you've buried your favorite horse, or tasted something sour?"

Julian paced to René's desk and took a seat, not bothering to remove his long coat. "Something doesn't feel right. The woman is keeping a secret from me."

René dropped the quill he had been holding and leaned backward in his chair. "Perhaps you're imagining problems where none exist. The daughters are chosen carefully. I promise you, they're good women. Or maybe, you clever bastard, this conversation hides a cunning strategy in the hopes of having your commander release you from your obligations."

"That statement could not be further from the truth."

"I'm glad to hear it. What are your suspicions? What could this woman be hiding?"

How did he answer that question? Maybe he read her character, her disposition, wrong. He tried to remember what disclosure had caused him concern. A sentiment incorrectly expressed, a reaction to his questioning he couldn't name. But they were strangers, perhaps they needed more time to become comfortable and more familiar with each other.

"I don't know." Julian snarled, rising from the chair. "I've questioned many men in my time, so I know when someone is misleading me. The woman is being dishonest."

"If it bothers you so much, choose another."

Julian stared at his hat, shifting it in his hands. "That's problematic."

"You'll have to elaborate."

Julian looked at René as if he might have the answers to assist his uneasiness, but his commander only stared at him perplexed. "I fancy the girl."

"You like her?" René chuckled, slapping his hand on the desk. "And that's a problem? Well, damn it anyway; I cannot believe I'm hearing this confession, especially given your feelings for Catherine."

"No more talk about Catherine. I now understand your viewpoint concerning my former flame. I confess it, she would never be happy in New France. This world requires stronger women."

"I'm glad you understand, finally."

"I have put her in my past, killing any feelings for her. We're two different people now."

"Is that so? Are you trying to convince yourself, or is this proclamation true?"

Julian's gut twisted thinking about Catherine and this choice that had been forced on him, forsaking his promise. Guilt consumed him for even considering a desirous woman like Madeleine.

"I would rather communicate my suspicions concerning Mademoiselle Madeleine."

"Seems to me you have two options," René offered, seeming surprised. "Press her for the truth, or let the dead stay buried until they rise to the surface with their secrets. Have you asked for a second meeting?"

"Yes, I have."

"When?"

"This afternoon. If the meeting goes well, I will ask for a marriage commitment. As I promised."

"Perhaps challenge her with a discussion of inquiry. And if you're satisfied with her confessions, kneel."

"I don't plan on bending the knee. We'll agree to sign a marriage contract and no more."

"Kneel," René emphasized, grinning. "Make your marriage request a demonstration of your affection, as such a display will assist with the next step. Women like a proposal."

A decision had been made but nothing had changed; Julian still felt nervous about the future, about tomorrow and the day after, but talking about the situation calmed his heavy heart.

"What of you, René? Has a woman caught your eye? Perhaps, Mademoiselle Louise?"

"We have a formal meeting of introduction tomorrow," he said with a wink.

"She's older. Does that concern you?"

"I appreciate a mature vintage. Wisdom comes with age, and I want a lady who can enlighten me with agreeable conversation. I admit; I've been lonely. I'm looking forward to the company."

"You may not prosper with children."

"She's not a relic, Julian. Let's leave this discussion for another day. Now that you're making a commitment, there's something else I want to discuss."

"What's that?"

René rose from his desk and walked to a cabinet. "A second proposal," he said with a shrug, retrieving a bottle of cognac from inside. "Our discussion will go down easier with a drink."

Julian didn't say anything. He watched René pour liquor into two cut-glass beakers. Approaching him, he passed a glass into his hands. What now?

"If you're agreeable to my proposition, there's a good bonus in it for you."

Julian tried to gauge René's expression. "I'm not going to like this."

"Likely not."

"Out with it, then."

"As you're aware, we've been constructing forts near Ville-Marie, further south along the confluence of la Rivière Richelieu. The construction of Fort Sainte-Anne is nearing completion."

"I'm aware of the work," Julian said, pondering the amber liquid, swirling it in the glass beaker. "I understand the reasons why, too."

"Smart man. Look, you're a second son. You'll never inherit your father's estate. I can assist your fortune, your future, by granting you a large piece of land. A plot near the mouth of la Rivière Richelieu would make you a wealthy man."

"Some men think land an opportune gift, but endowments come with a fee. Your motives are clever."

"You're no fool. This is why I chose you for the work." René smiled, saluting him. "We must protect our land, our natural resources and our people. Strong men and women must see the work through."

"And granting myself and other officers land in the South, in this area, does what? I want to hear you say it."

"Honestly, Julian, there's no need to hide the truth. Having patrols on this stretch of river serves to protect our colony from Iroquois attacks, and perhaps a British invasion. I will not delude you; the work will be difficult. Should you choose to accept this mission, your sacrifice will reimburse you doubly when your tour of duty is complete."

Julian sighed, shifting his hat in his hands. These were dangerous times. In his estimation, every part of this new world held reasons to cause a man distress, but it was his responsibility to try and make this land safer. Now a commander was handing him a feminine complication. How could he take a new wife into a dangerous territory, risking her welfare? But maybe the risk was worth the reward. René was right. He'd never gain a seigneury in his homeland. No choice but to accept the offer for the betterment of two individuals' futures.

"I will accept the land grant, I would be a fool not to, but it's hardly a gift putting myself and my new bride in danger. Fort Sainte-Anne is the furthest fortification south of Fort Richelieu and as such is the most at risk of attack. The Iroquois, the Mohawk especially, see the waterway as theirs. They will lay claim to their traditional hunting grounds."

"We're all in danger, at war until a peace agreement can be made. If the situation should weaken, well, this is why I need you to travel to Fort Sainte-Anne."

Julian saw he had no other choice. If he married Madeleine, he risked her well-being. *What should he do?* A soldier's life came with complex responsibilities. Perhaps it was better if he didn't tell her everything.

"Which men will come with me?"

"Mack Chovier, for one. His knowledge of aboriginal movements and his skill for tracking will assist you. He will join your team at Fort Richelieu. I'll send other officers to defend the new fort, too. Perhaps Gauvain, he's a quirky fellow, but a good officer."

"Do I have any say in the matter? Taking a wife into Iroquois territory is a fool's business. Maybe we should postpone the wedding."

"No, you will not weasel out of your commitment. Focus on the task at hand. The British colonies are growing at a fast pace, and we must protect our stake, our land. We are at threat of war from one side, and attack from the other. This makes good sense to do."

"As far as I'm concerned, we could be spreading our forces too thin, risking attack at Ville de Québec. I agree with the judgment call, but I do not have to like it."

"You understand your responsibilities well enough and you've never shirked them before. Focus on what you'll gain, a large property near la Rivière Richelieu. When the risk is past, you can retire. Farm the land if you choose to do so. I understand it's fertile."

Julian stood, placing his slouch hat on his head. "This will come as a shock to Mademoiselle Madeleine, should I take her as my bride."

"She may be your responsibility, but she doesn't have to know about your mission. Get out of here." René chortled, slugging another shot of cognac. "Every woman wants to hitch her wagon to an officer. Now go, learn her secrets. Sell your bride on a new home."

Julian finished his cognac in one hard swallow. It warmed his throat but was a bitter elixir going down. "If I must."

"Until our borders are safe, Captain, not one of us rests easy. But if we're to remain in this new world, each one of us must do the work to keep it safe."

"I'll do my part. I always have."

"You're a man who can bear the load. That's why I entrusted you to carry out this mission."

CHAPTER 12

*M*adeleine sat on an armchair inside the bedchamber she shared with Marie. She glanced at her friend who lounged on her bed, preparing for male suitors by reading a book about etiquette and social graces. Unmindful of lessons a lady might receive from the pages of a book, Madeleine remembered her father's timepiece lectures on living a good and honest life.

My daughter, show your respect. Act with modesty. Always conduct yourself as a lady—

She might have achieved his expectations had her father survived his plague, but his death had forced her to adapt to a different type of norm, surviving life on the *rue de la tristesse*. *The selfish fool.* She might have faced disownment had the gambler known of her choices, the decisions she had been forced to make because of his stupidity, but now an opportunity for a better life was being presented. *An officer.* She was prepared to hold the torch of dishonesty if that meant gaining more freedom. Lying didn't seem right, but what other choice did she have?

A knock sounded against the door, followed by Sister Abby entering the room. "Captain Julian Benoit is here to see you, Madeleine," she said, seeming irritated. "Please prepare yourself for a journey. The captain will escort you into the country."

"Alone, without a chaperone?"

"It's not to my liking," she complained, pursing her lips. "But Captain Benoit assures me that he will be a proper gentleman and guide you appropriately."

Madeleine gazed at Marie, raising her eyebrows. "I'm not sure I'm comfortable with the change of plans," she said, addressing Sister Abby.

"You can refuse him. It's your right."

Madeleine swallowed. She had no choice but to accept. "Tell Captain Benoit, I'll meet with him shortly."

Madeleine waited until the sister had left their company, and then gestured to Marie. "I didn't expect he'd return so soon. What should I do?"

Marie closed her book and placed it on her lap. "Present yourself accordingly. Style your hair, smooth out your skirts, and put a smile on your pretty face. After all, your fatted cow has arrived. I hope when my gentleman escort arrives, I have the courage to drink the milk, and every gesture appears sincere."

Madeleine rose from the armchair and checked her appearance in the looking glass, touching her cheek. She preened herself, brushing her hair and coiling it into a bun atop her head. After pinning the layers, she placed a cream bonnet on her head. "Sister Abby seemed upset. He's escorting me without a chaperone."

"He's a captain. Such a role comes with its privileges."

"What if he attempts to do something indiscreet? What if... he attempts a kiss?"

Marie giggled where she lay on the bed. "You're not a virgin, Maddie. If he asked me, I'd kiss him."

Madeleine's cheeks flamed. Though the day was warm, she grabbed a woolen wrap and prepared to leave the bedchamber, but she turned to face her friend. "It's not a badge of honor I've been forced to wear." She cautioned, pursing her lips, frowning. "I'd change the past if I could."

"True enough, what woman wouldn't in your position, but some men cherish experience."

Madeleine flushed with humiliation, contemplating her friend with suspicion, squeezing her hand into a fist. "I'd much rather be a virginal bride with no sense of the pains to come."

"The sexual act only hurts the first time, or so I've been told."

"Perhaps so, but planted seeds carry their own weight, a woman doesn't hold such burdens with pride."

Marie rose and approached Madeleine at the door. She grasped her chin and tipped it upward. "A rotten fate was forced on you. You didn't ask for the abuse, but since you have this burden, be bold in your recovery. Walk on, dear Madeleine. Hold your head high."

"You continue to surprise me with your wit, your strength even, but my suitor waits for me. I'll see you when I return."

Madeleine grasped the door handle, but pausing, turned

to Marie. "I have never had a friend like you. You give me the strength to walk through this doorway with my heart beating a little stronger. I appreciate your support. Marie, I wish you were my sister."

"I'd like that," she said, breaking into a huge grin. "I only have brothers. But it's best you make your way below. Good luck, sister."

Madeleine gave Marie a quick hug, passed through the upper corridor, then carefully descended a ladder to the lower floor, soon walking to the front parlor wearing her mulberry dress and carrying a cream woolen shawl, ready to travel wherever the captain took her, but not ready to confide the truth. He waited for her near the entrance.

Captain Benoit was every bit as handsome as the day before, standing at the front door with his slouch hat held in his hands. His broad shoulders and strong arms could be her answering shelter. A light within his hazel eyes promised something new. She could not help but smile as she approached him.

"A good day to you, Mademoiselle Bourbonnais."

"And to you, Captain." She lowered her gaze demurely, seeking the notice of his hazel eyes. "I understand you're escorting me into the country."

He offered his elbow, and she placed her gloved hand atop his upper arm. "I have obtained permission to give you an idea of where we might live, should marriage be a mutually agreeable option for the two of us."

"I will be alone with you?"

"Does that disturb you?"

"Not at all." Madeleine giggled nervously, raising her eyebrows. "It's only that Sister Abby…"

"Yes." He grinned, leading her through the front doors. "She was insistent we not depart alone. Proper decorum of a young lady and such."

"And you will not disappoint, and will conduct yourself as a gentleman?"

"You'll find I'm well mannered," he said with a wink, escorting her down two steps.

She didn't respond to his comment as he led her to a horse-drawn carriage, where two well-muscled Canadian Bay horses waited. She stopped by their flanks, stepping apart from Julian, to stroke the nearest sooty brown coat. The animals flicked their tails in response to the flies. She considered the day was hot.

"Please assist me," she beseeched. He grasped her fingers, and even through her gloves she felt his warmth as he assisted her to rise from the mounting steps to the box seat. Once she sat comfortably, he climbed up, jostling the carriage, and took a seat beside her.

"Are you ready?" he asked, staring at her with an inquisitive expression.

"Perhaps, I think so."

He flicked the reins, urging the mares to a trot, contemplating her with a serious expression that caused her to fear what questions might come next.

"Why did you cross the ocean?" Julian asked. He glanced away as they rounded a curve, and then faced her again. "It's a difficult journey, especially for a woman. Did you do it to receive the king's monetary gift? Or was there some other reason?"

"You get right to the point." Madeleine took a deep breath, choosing not to reply in an unhurried fashion. "New France offered a new hope for my future. The king's gift, a generous dowry of fifty livres coupled with the paid fare, is a lot of money for a woman such as I. It was a contributing factor to have a better life."

"You said you were living at the Hôpital Général. How did the hospital become your home?"

Madeleine turned away, feeling the sun's heat on her forehead. She swallowed, squirming beneath his scrutiny. He didn't trust her. She had to make him trust her. She gazed at him, facing his inquiry.

"It wasn't a home. I was removed from a Parisian street by a night watchman."

"Why?"

"Well, if truth be told, the aristocracy does not appreciate orphans defiling their streets. And Julian, I did impart my family's sad fate. My father. My mother. After their death, I was thrown from my house and into the street. I had no place to go. No kind relations to assist me. I take no pleasure in my past and what I must confide. I will say only this once and then never again as reliving the past is simply too painful."

"Go on. If your answer satisfies me, I'll never ask such questions again."

Madeleine scrutinized his expression, hoping he would understand. "Have you ever been hungry?"

"I've been hungry. Who hasn't?"

"I don't think you have, at least not in the way I have." Madeleine broached the subject, nibbling at her lip. "Have you been forced to search for a place to sleep at the end of the day, *hungry and afraid*, scouring the streets for food, begging for someone, *anyone*, to spare a bite of bread?"

"No," he replied, slapping the reins against the horses, "I have not faced such dire circumstances."

"When a passer-by would not yield their bread to me, I simply snatched it from their hands and ran. Have you ever stooped so low?"

"Cannot say I have ever stolen from those richer than me. Have you had to beg for anything other than food? Such regrettable action leads me to question your nightly lodgings and what price you might have accepted for a bed. Please, answer honestly."

MADELEINE APPEARED SHOCKED, perhaps even frightened by the question, which led Julian to wonder if he had struck a nerve. Her face turned a brilliant shade of scarlet. She tried to speak, her lips moved, quivered slightly, but whatever she might have said shied away to silence.

Julian stopped the carriage. He gazed at her vulnerability. If he were not careful, he would pay for this moment for the rest of his life.

"What are you insinuating?" she finally asked.

He knew he had to push. Marriage was an important step. He had to ensure she was the right woman. "You're not being honest with me. Maybe you found a place to rest for the night? Maybe with a man?"

"Hah!" she gasped, appearing as if she might cry. Either

the sun or her own shame caused her cheeks to flame red. "Such boldness in your inquiry, I cannot answer your question."

"Cannot, or will not?"

She closed her eyes, took a deep breath. "I see what you imply, Monsieur, but I'm not a prostitute."

"It's all right, save your appeal. Your expression validates my suspicions that your virginity is not intact. However, this might come as a surprise to you, but I can live with the fact you've been with another man."

He watched her eyes pool with water. "I don't expect you to understand, but…let me try to explain. I was an orphan on the street."

"I understand you fell on tough times, but is it necessary for an orphan to fall into the arms of needy men? How could you lower yourself? You've said it yourself, you come from a good family."

Tears slipped from her amber eyes. Julian saw she attempted to swipe them away. "I have made difficult decisions. I'm embarrassed to admit one of those choices was being forced to lie with a social miscreant, who I might add, was extremely grateful to take advantage of my situation."

"I'm sorry you faced hardship."

"I," she said, taking a deep quivering breath, "take no comfort in the act of choosing between right and wrong, nor did I find any pleasure in the gentleman who used me. A lady does not relish having to lower herself to such humiliating life lessons."

"Was there someone specific?" he asked, his tone soft.

She looked away, gulping through her pain. Julian saw how she tried to control her emotion. "Yes."

"Who?"

She turned to face him. "My father left this world without the benefit of paying his gambling debts. One of his creditors was extremely happy to have me pay for my father's negligence. One aristocrat in particular…"

"Took advantage of your situation," Julian said, rising quickly to anger, and surprisingly, wanting to meet the gentleman at dawn. "The bastard."

"Turn this carriage around," Madeleine shrieked. "Return me to my lodgings at once. I hardly expect you to make a commitment to a woman who has been soiled by another man."

"Was it of your own choosing, or is this a well-made story?"

"Of my choosing?" She screeched, her voice rising. "What woman would willingly accept such a fate? How dare you question my sincerity; I freely confessed my downfall. If you had been in my place, you would not ask such insulting questions."

"Are you with child?" He pressed further.

"Am I what?" She gasped, sucking in a breath. "Goodness, no!"

He reached forward and grasped her hand. "By the grace of God."

"I assure you, Madeleine, you will never have to beg for my protection or my care. I will not force myself on you either. Should we marry, that is."

She glanced away, looking to a place he could not see. "Presently, I don't see how marriage could be possible."

Julian ignored the comment. "I'd like to show you a property in the country. The type of home where we might live, should we agree to pursue a life together."

"Are you certain?" she said through her tears. "After the scandalous exposé I've been forced to divulge?"

"I have yet to make a decision," he said, urging the iron mares forward. "I'm not sure why I'm accepting this tell-tale narrative. Most men would not."

"I don't know what to say."

"Don't say anything. We start on an equal footing, for neither am I an innocent."

"An experienced gentleman, then?"

"Time will tell if I can satisfy."

Julian contemplated Madeleine; she could not regard him directly after the disclosure. She was a beauty. He understood why men would take advantage of her, why he might yet, too.

Still, she held a secret. He peered at her belly, well hidden beneath her linen gown. Had she lied to him? Was she expecting? She had voiced a firm rejection, but her quiet resolve nagged at him. He gazed at where her hands lay folded in her lap.

She certainly must know after three months at sea. Could he live with the truth if it were so? He should do as she asked and return her to the boarding house, but still he drove the horses forward. This new world required strong women, and to bear what she had suffered, there was no doubt in his mind she would satisfy in this regard.

THE JOURNEY to the manor house took longer than Madeleine expected. They left the comfort of Ville de Québec for the rural countryside, the horse-drawn carriage traveling beside a trail of grassy spikes and yellow primrose flowers, the land edged with a border of tall maple trees. She had lied to Julian about her condition and knew he might catch her in her web of duplicity. At some point, she must confess the truth. Where would that leave her? He was a captain in the regiment and she, despite the fact she had been born into an aristocratic family, was no more than a Parisian shrew. *A harlot. An expectant orphan.* Could she deceive a good man to protect her unborn child? If she determined to confess the truth, what then, disaster?

After traveling some distance, Julian stopped the rig near a rectangular manor house built beside a slow meandering waterway. Madeleine admitted straight away that the stone dwelling set on a rolling prairie seemed divine. Four casement windows were set in the southern exposure, with three dormer windows situated above them and nestled inside a steep roof. It was a pretty sight. Much better than anything she could have expected.

"We could own a home and land similar to this," Julian said, his expression serious, holding the reins against his lap, and soon stopping the carriage. "I have accepted a land grant, a seigneurial distribution near Fort Richelieu. We could never afford such a gift in our homeland, but the parcel would come with a steep price."

"Why does the cost concern you?"

"If we agree to marry, I will farm the land after my tour of duty is complete."

"A home, though you don't seem happy to speak of it."

"The gift is not what it seems," he mused aloud, staring at her intently. "It appears well and good in theory, a location perfectly set, the promise of a home, the property our king and country has chosen for us. A gift in compensation for our marital sacrifice. If we decide to take this step together."

"Simply for choosing to marry?"

"Yes."

"A generous gift. Is this why you accept the hand of a stranger and contemplate marriage, for the benefit of a home? A plot of land?"

Julian placed the reins on the dashboard and then climbed down from the carriage, taking some time to reply to her question. He paced to her side of the carriage, then offered his hand, soon assisting her to the ground.

"I have chosen to reside in this new world. I accept my tour of duty. I do as I'm bid. I never supposed that an officer's duty might include marriage."

Madeleine considered Julian's statement while contemplating the open space. The horses whinnied and the wind blew, sending tall grasses swishing back and forth. A cold shiver crawled up her spine and she pulled her wrap around her shoulders. "There's something you're not telling me."

"Is my position that clear?"

"I have shared my past. Don't you think you should oblige me as truthfully?"

"Will it make a difference?"

"Maybe it's time I asked the questions, Captain. What do you keep from me?"

He took her arm and led her toward the stone manor's front entrance. "Let's speak of confessions inside. I see that you're cold."

"I suspect I'll be colder still once you tell me the truth."

He frowned, then took a deep breath. "Perhaps the news will go easier if I can satisfy your needs by ensuring your comfort, offering shelter from the prevailing winds. I'll start a fire once we're inside the dwelling."

Madeleine walked beside Julian, being careful where she stepped on the hard-packed ground. Once they neared the house, Julian grasped the brass handle, pushed the door open, released her arm, and then gestured for her to precede him inside.

Once she had passed through the doorway, Madeleine considered the home, reflecting on a haven she hadn't experienced in some time. A great room featured a large brick and mortar fireplace, a couple cabinets, a wooden table; and surprisingly, a fresh bouquet of white wildflowers resting in the middle of the tabletop. She stepped forward, taking a daisy from the vase. She saw Julian was watching her as she held the delicate petals to her nose.

"Who would be so kind?"

Julian smiled at her while preparing jute kindling in the hearth. "Perhaps, Kiah, Mack's wife. She's from the Wendat tribe."

"Who?"

He stopped his fire preparation to peer at her. "A friend and colleague, Mack has many skills, but he prefers the life of a fur trapper. He met Kiah when he began trading furs. They fell in love. Because of his kindness, and likely the subsequent trading gifts to the tribe, the chief permitted them to marry."

Madeleine retrieved a side chair and sat beside the wooden table, dismissing the comment. "I've told you my truth, Julian. What of you; why do you search for a ready-made wife?"

"I didn't ask for marriage," he muttered, taking a striker and striking the flint, causing sparks to fly into a nest. "You're a beautiful woman, but the truth is, I didn't want a commitment."

He left his work once the fire caught and sat on the opposite chair. Comfortable, he didn't look away from her scrutiny. Merely waited for more questions to come.

"Why are we here, at this place?"

"The idea of marriage was forced on me by my commanding officer," he said, keeping a straight face and offering no emotion.

"There's more to your confession. What do you leave unsaid?"

"'Tis nothing."

"Tell me," she said, glancing downward, feeling white petals slide like silk between her fingers, "I've confided my truth."

"I don't want to hurt you, but there was another woman in my life," he said with a grimace, sighing, glancing away. "A woman I promised to make a commitment to when I returned to France."

"And yet here you are in my company. Why did you entertain the possibility of becoming my husband when your heart lies with another? I see that..." Madeleine took a deep breath. "You still love her."

"I won't deny it," Julian said, resuming his regard. "I begged her to come to New France when I chose to remain in this country. She would not come."

"I understand the refusal, having made the journey. But for a man such as you, I would have made the sacrifice. Who is this woman?"

His expression brightened at her comment. "I'd rather not say. It hardly matters, anyway."

Madeleine placed the daisy on the table and then reached across the expanse and laid her fingers on his knuckles. She massaged the digits, knowing the contact would not relieve his pain. "If such a man had begged for my company, I would have crossed a sea of sorrows to touch his hand. I'm sorry for your discomfort."

He smiled, ever so slimly. "You seem like a good woman, Madeleine, despite your sad past. But before you enter into a marriage contract with me, there's something I need to tell you."

"You can tell me."

"I'm being sent to Fort Sainte-Anne to guard against attacks from our enemies."

"The enemy?" she asked, pulling her hand away, her eyes registering her surprise.

"The Iroquois Nation."

"Who might these people be?"

"An indigenous people, the first people of this land. They fight for the control of the beaver trade from a land they feel belongs to them."

"Would we be safe?"

"Something for you to consider before you agree to marriage."

"Why should I fear them?"

"The warriors are brave; and ruthless with their enemies."

"Do we go alone?"

"No," Julian said, rising from his chair. "We would be accompanied by other officers and their wives, should they also agree to marry. Mack will join us at Fort Richelieu, so you would meet him."

"I will be in danger." Madeleine shivered. Despite the fire burning in the hearth, she pulled her wrap tighter around her shoulders.

"I will not sugar-coat this. You must know the truth."

"Will you protect me, keep me safe from harm?" she said, swallowing, fearing the troubles that could lie ahead.

She watched Julian rise from his chair and kneel, soon grasping her hand. "I don't know what the future holds or if we'll ever love each other, but I can promise to protect you, if you can accept the challenges to come. Madeleine, will you marry me?"

Astonished, surprised even, she slipped to her knees on the floor. She gripped his arms and gazed into his eyes. Earnestly, he waited for her reply.

"Yes," she said, breathing a sigh of relief, though she had little choice in the matter. Julian's proposal was the answer to her prayers, and she liked the way his face brightened with the acceptance of his offer. A light brightened his eyes.

"I will be your wife."

CHAPTER 13

"'Tis my wedding day," Madeleine said to Marie, while staring at her reflection in the oak standing mirror. "You have styled me into a princess. I cannot remember a time when I have looked so beautiful or felt so special. Who stares at me from inside this mirror?"

"A bride. A *fille du Roi,* a daughter a king and country would be proud to call their own."

"Mrs. Madeleine Benoit," she verbalized aloud, "an officer's wife."

She fingered a crown of white daisies circling her forehead, scrutinized her chestnut hair artfully pulled from her forehead and expertly weaved into a plaited chignon. An ivory satin wedding gown was squared at the neckline, slightly exposing the rise of her breasts and the creamy curve of her shoulder. The fabric extended over a wide farthingale trimmed with a delicate array of floral petals of white lace, which drew her eye downward to her satin feet.

"My life is about to change and these niceties, these

flowers, this beautiful dress, cannot conceal who I am inside. Why do I feel so terrible?"

"Do not say such a thing, not on your wedding day. You're a beautiful woman, inside and out."

"I have only been in this country for four days. This is happening too fast. I'm marrying a stranger out of desperation. *Do I want this submission?* I did not dream of deceiving a man, regardless that your presentation is flawless."

"Maddie, please be positive," Marie soothed, stepping closer to the mirror. "Keep to your faith and the convictions you hold."

"I admire your faith in me," Madeleine said, turning away from the mirror. "Despite your master skill on fashioning me into an enchanted creature, guilt is taking hold. I'm having second thoughts. Marie, marrying the captain is wrong on so many levels. Can I burden the good man with my lot?"

"What other choice do you have at this late hour? If you tell the captain the truth and he shuns you, no other man will have you."

"True enough," Madeleine said, slumping into the armchair with a whoosh of satin skirt. "But I could show him my respect through my honest appeal."

"A change in course could lead to disaster. Think of my handiwork that would be for naught."

Rising to the compliment, Madeleine smiled and placed her hand on her belly, sensing the baby stirring again, as if the child had some say in the matter. "I shall get through this." She shook her head, sighing. "But I'm not sure how."

"Maybe I can lift your spirits. I have something for you,"

Marie said, passing a wrapped piece of satin cloth. "It will brighten your spirits. Make you feel better."

Madeleine accepted the package, neatly tied with a satin ribbon, but she took her time unwrapping it, stunned and appreciative. "Marie, this is kind of you."

"Do not stare. Open it."

She unwrapped the cloth and saw a metal work of tiny silver leaves and dainty white flowers. "'Tis beautiful. But..."

"The necklet represents innocence and purity."

"I cannot accept this. I'm neither." She tried to return it, shaking her head.

"Don't say such a thing!" Marie blurted, her tone sharp. She grasped Madeleine's hand and squeezed the bridal gift inside her palm. "Your heart is pure, your soul is innocent, despite the man, the men who have wronged you."

"You are too kind, I could cry."

"Not on your wedding day! You will rise to this occasion, to your new life, and I will place this necklet against your fair skin. It will draw the captain's gaze from your décolletage to your sweet neck, to your lovely amber eyes."

"Sweet Marie, I shall not want for another woman's friendship," she said with a grin, rising from the armchair.

"Turn around."

She did so, and soon sensed kind fingers and cold metal against her neck. "Who gave you this precious gift, Marie?"

"It belonged to my grand-mère. 'Twas the last item my mother placed in my hand before we said our goodbyes at the port of La Rochelle."

"Before you boarded the ship?" Madeleine mused, turning

to her friend. "You cannot give me this. It's a family heirloom."

"But now, we are family," Marie asserted, squeezing her fingers, "sisters."

Madeleine hugged her friend. "I will return it after the ceremony. I'll wear it with honor and with pride."

A knock at the door caused them each to start. Sister Abby stepped inside the room. She smiled, contemplating the bride.

"The carriage has arrived," she said with a grin. "The time has come to leave for the church."

Marie squeezed her hand. "Are you ready?"

Madeleine nodded, pursing her lips, but she wasn't sure of anything.

MADELEINE LEFT HER BEDCHAMBER, accompanied by Marie, her matron of honor. She walked along the corridor, her long white train sliding on the hardwood floor, soon descending a narrow ladder. At the front entrance, the women who had accompanied her across the ocean waited for her to make her appearance.

She paused on the final rung, reflecting on their faces. A serene expression seemed to envelop them, shared whimsical smiles, as if they dreamed of being where she stood.

If only they knew.

Geneviève stepped forward. "You make a beautiful bride, Madeleine. The officer is a fortunate man."

"Thank you," she said, having no further words as the

daughters enveloped her, congratulating her. Sister Abby opened the front door and beckoned her to walk to the waiting carriage.

Marie grabbed her hand, smiling, acknowledging her worries with a wink but supporting her choice to continue to the altar. Sister Abby escorted the pair as they progressed from the boarding house, crossed a brief expanse of cobblestones and climbed into the carriage. Once they were seated, the driver clucked his tongue and the iron horses gave way, trotting toward the church.

The other daughters left the boarding house and walked behind the carriage. Their grand parade soon arrived at the Cathedral-Basilica of Notre-Dame, the church where Madeleine would marry.

INSIDE THE CATHEDRAL, Captain Julian Benoit stood nervously at the altar waiting for his bride, his commander standing beside him. Uncomfortable in his groom's clothing, he worried René had tied his cravat too tight. His embroidered vest, black waistcoat and white breeches fit him well, and he hoped his bride would be impressed.

Gazing at the assembled guests, most of whom were fellow officers, he swayed on his booted feet, waiting.

"You're digging a hole in the flooring, Julian. More nervous than the bride, I suspect."

"A bride who keeps me waiting. I'm tired of waiting. Do you have the ring?"

"You've asked me the question at least a dozen times,"

René said with a grin, pulling the gold band from his pocket. "See for yourself, your seal of commitment is right here. Safe and sound."

"Good. Lose it and the deal is off."

"You're at the altar. There's no turning back now."

A conductor in the choral loft raised his hands and with a flash of bravo, instructed the orchestra of ten men to begin. Julian glanced at the group, fancying how the slide of a bow across strings could create such a tranquil vibration. The violin's sweet melody coupled with a resonant and haunting bass came together perfectly. He waited patiently, listening to the rise of his own nervousness and the sweet pluck of heartstrings. A sudden sigh from the congregation, and Julian turned to see his bride. In awe of her beauty, he swallowed.

Mademoiselle Madeleine Bourbonnais walked toward the nave with her matron of honor assisting with the trailing veil. At the back of the church, she paused, parallel to the pews, and stared in Julian's direction.

He took a deep breath. Was she the woman he had agreed to marry? He swallowed again. Having never seen a woman so fetching, so fascinating, not even his Catherine compared to her beauty.

Julian was disappointed when the matron of honor made her appearance first and slowly walked up the lengthy aisle. He dismissed her pretty face, her brunette hair and rouged lips, as he was anxious for his bride to come to him.

I have waited so long for a moment such as this...

The bride started to take her walk. She lowered her head demurely, taking her first step along the length of the aisle. The congregation rose, all eyes on the bride, but her attention was solely focused on him. Step touch step, she waltzed closer, in time to the music. All alone, without the benefit of a father's arm to lend a guiding support, or a mother's love to advise or acknowledge her commitment.

Poor petite soul, he felt sorry for her.

Julian sensed her nervousness as she bridged the distance between them, witnessing her momentary glances, the gentle rise of her chest and swell of her bosom above the square neckline of her dress. He closed his eyes temporarily, thinking how long it had been since coupling with a woman.

She will be mine, my wife.

When she breached the distance, he extended his hand, and she placed her white-gloved fingers into his grip. Her breath quivered from her lips. She lowered her head and greeted his expression with a sweet smile.

He pulled her close, his lips feathering across her earlobe. "You are the most beautiful woman I have ever laid eyes upon. Welcome to our wedding day." He kissed her ear, grasping her arm, guiding her nearer to the priest.

"Dearly beloved," the Father said with his hand on the bible. "We are gathered here together, in the sight of God and in the presence of these witnesses, to join together this man and this woman, in holy matrimony."

Julian gazed at Madeleine, witnessing her fearful expression. He squeezed her fingers, trying to calm her.

"Julian?" the priest called to him. "Love your wife as you would love the church. Bestow on her many blessings, which the Lord hath taught you. Patience, kindness, your protection, and trust, as 1st Corinthians has taught the Lord's children, love is realized when one is patient."

"Madeleine," the priest reiterated. "Love your husband as you would love the church. Bestow on him many blessings, which the Lord hath taught you. Patience, kindness, your hope and truth, as love is realized when God's children are open and honest."

He gazed at them. "Is it 'your will' to marry?"

"Yes," they each whispered.

"A marriage is not entered into lightly, but reverently. Therefore, I encourage you to come together, each to the other, as one flesh."

"Julian, behold your bride. Will you take this woman as your wedded wife?"

"I will," he said softly.

"Madeleine, behold your groom. Will you take this man as your wedded husband?"

MADELEINE DIDN'T RESPOND. The priest's words of truth and honesty weighed heavily on her conscience. The silence lingered, stretched—the priest waited for her answering pledge. The assembled guests waited for her response too, and when she didn't speak, the whispering began. Julian regarded her with curiosity.

Marie stepped forward and whispered in her ear: "*Madeleine…*"

The baby moved.

"Madeleine?" the priest asked again. "Will you take this man as your husband?"

Her face surely crumpled. She felt like she was sinking

inside herself. Her face flushed with heat and her heartbeat quickened. Julian stepped closer to her side. "What's wrong?"

"Julian," she whispered, feeling faint. "I must speak to you."

"After our vows have been spoken," he replied, squeezing her hand. "And not before."

"It will be too late…"

He disregarded her comment. "Anything you have to say can wait. For better or worse—" he whispered, squeezing her fingers. "Father, ask her again."

"Will you take this man as your wedded husband?"

She held his hands; she gazed into his hazel eyes, seeing he would not wait for a response much longer.

"I will—" she vowed, hastening her promise and trusting him to protect her. She was certain the congregation applauded in relief.

She promised to love him in sickness and in health, until death did they part. He placed a simple band of gold on her ring finger, and she did likewise for her new husband.

"Julian, you may kiss your bride."

Stepping close, he clutched her face in his hands, while she stood before him like a frightened doe. He smiled serenely, soon kissing her lips. Pulling away, delighting in the moment of their first kiss, she saw his face shining with joy. The kiss was clearly a favored moment of the nuptials and the guests responded to the affection with quick applause. The priest smiled, seemingly pleased with the two lives he had brought together.

"I announce thee as man and wife. What God brings

together, let no man put asunder. Please welcome Mr. and Mrs. Benoit."

The orchestra struck a chord. Julian offered her his arm and she placed her hand on his strength. "Shall we, mine wife?"

Madeleine nodded, smiling slimly, permitting her new husband to take the lead. Later he would question what had been left unsaid at the altar. What would he do when he learned her secret? Would he insist on an annulment? For now, the repercussions could wait.

CHAPTER 14

The bells pealed, swinging, metal striking metal, caroling to the celebrants who stood outside the church on the cobblestoned square of La Place-Royale. Standing near the front stoop, Julian Benoit listened to the merry din while contemplating the woman who stood by his side. Still a stranger, with the acceptance of the words, *I will*, she had become his wife. Seeking her attention, he stared at her, reflecting on her beauty. When she noticed his perusal, she smiled timidly. He grasped her hand, squeezing her gloved fingers, attempting to reassure whatever fears furrowed her brow.

A receiving line soon formed of daughters, fellow officers, and Ville de Québec residents to wish them a happy marriage. Julian waited patiently for each guest to extend his or her kind regards. However, their congratulations could wait. He only wanted to take his leave from festivity, remove his bride to their home and begin a new life together.

It had been a long time since Julian had touched a woman

in a physical way. For more than a year he had been loyal, *to Catherine*, but such passions to his wife might have to wait. Madeleine might not permit him to satisfy his needs.

She had already hesitated at the altar, but her moment of pause could only be a brief interlude of a bride's shyness. A moment of hesitation should not spoil their wedding day.

"Are you happy?" he asked her when the greetings were long past while guiding her to the waiting carriage.

"Yes," she whispered, eyeing him nervously, then glancing away.

"Then why does your face pinch as if you have tasted a sour piece of fruit? Does it concern you that I might offend your modesty?"

"I'm sorry," she said with a wince. "I don't mean to upset you, but our marriage is new. I need time to adapt to this new life."

"I imagine I'll need an equal period of adjustment. If it's shyness you're feeling, I can be shy as well."

"You, shy?" She smiled pleasantly, her raised lips revealing perfect white teeth. "I thought with your role as an officer, you'd be more outgoing. Frankly, a reserved manner surprises me, Julian."

He pressed closer to her as they approached the carriage. "Well, not exactly shy, per se, I can be bold when it comes to matters of the heart," he gazed at her meaningfully, "if you lead me well."

She blushed, lowering her gaze. "What do you mean?"

"Madeleine," he hinted, coaxing her forward, grasping her gloved fingers, assisting her inside the carriage. "Let me be clear, certainly our marriage is not a love match, but we could show each other some comfort and mutual affection in time. Yes? Perhaps tonight, if you're agreeable."

"Tonight?" She breathed, wincing as he assisted her to the bench seat, her ivory skirts amassing around her legs.

A year had passed since Julian had lain with a woman. He missed the affection and the tenderness that a couple could court in each other's arms, but beholding his wife's crestfallen expression, he supposed his period of drought would continue. They had known each other for a brief time. He assured himself, an adjustment period was necessary.

"I understand your concern," he began, taking his seat, "but every bride must accept her husband." Once they were seated, he gestured to her with his hand. "And rest assured, I would never hurt you. I am a patient man."

"A good man," she said, briefly studying the leather bench seat. "I don't believe you would hurt me, not intentionally."

He grasped her gloved hand, and pressed forward, edging closer to his bride. "As an officer of the Carignan-Salières Regiment, I'm paid to protect the settlement. I assure you," he vocalized with a firm tone, squeezing her fingers. "I will safeguard my wife. Furthermore, I have never hurt a woman in my life. I have no intention of starting now."

"Julian, we have spoken our vows before God and countrymen, yet we are strangers to each other."

"Is that what upsets you?" Julian asked, imagining her beneath him in their bed. "That I might desire my new wife? You're not a virginal maid, and every couple first meets as strangers, regardless of the courtship period."

Madeleine's eyes widened in shock. She turned from him, her cheeks blushing pink, as if his speech on human sensuality had been shocking. He forced himself to release his grip. Her rejection bruised his pride. Julian hadn't meant to be unkind. He wanted his new wife. He pulled her close, compelling her attention. It surprised him, how much he wanted to know her charm.

"My virginity was stolen from me," she blurted in a rush of words. "A forced copulation hurt and shamed me; I never want such care of a man again."

"You were raped?"

She looked at him then, contemplating his expression, her face crumpling. He watched the emotion build in her amber eyes. He didn't speak, permitting her scrutiny.

"I will kill the bastard if I ever meet him. You only need to point him out to me, but I'm your husband. You cannot fear I would be equally rough, and hurt you, too?"

"Julian, I cannot face this."

He retrieved her hand, gripped it tight, and tipped her face to his earnestness as the carriage pulled away, proceeding along the Rue Sous le Fort. "Look, mine wife, you must not be afraid of your husband. I will not impose my physical wants on you until you're ready to receive my attention. I'm no monster. I do not beg. Until you want my affection, I will not force myself on you. No man should ever force himself on a woman."

"You're serious. You would wait until I'm comfortable? But this is our wedding night, and Sister Abby informed me I must…"

"You bend to your husband's will now." Julian grinned, hoping. "It's customary for the bride and groom to consummate their marriage on their wedding night, but if you're timid, or frightened? I don't want my wife afraid of me. I want my wife… well, charmed by my touch. Time, chérie, is what we require."

The carriage reached the end of the street and soon climbed a steep hill. Julian released Madeleine, disappointed, but placed his hand near her thigh, thinking it wise she become accustomed to his proximity and his touch. He leaned against the backrest, enjoying the jostling and the clicking sound of the horses' hooves as they passed across the cobbles.

"Most men would not wait," he heard her say. "Most men would…"

"I'm not most men," he said, patting her thigh, "I'm your husband."

The first hint of a smile played on her face. "Where will we retire for the night?"

"Hopefully," he hinted, his demeanor becoming desirous, "in my bed."

Her facial expression became panicked, again. "You implied you would wait?"

He stroked her gown-covered leg with his fingertips. "I didn't say I would not touch you; touch is something you must grow accustomed to."

"Oh," she murmured, shooting him a warning look.

He leaned closer, grasping her waist, daring to kiss her lips. She permitted him to do so, eyeing him with a degree of curiosity. He took her quiet behavior as a promising sign and pressed his advantage.

"Especially," he whispered, kissing her lips again, "when the contact comes from your husband."

MADELEINE SUCKED IN A SHOCKED BREATH. Julian had kissed her lips, had dared to touch her thickening waist. Had he guessed the truth? Had he noticed the roundness of her belly? She swallowed, worrying, knowing this secret could not hold much longer. Scrutinizing his expression, she searched for any hint of recognition. Sweet Lord, guilt clutched at her heart when he smiled, his response curious.

She was saved from further investigation when the carriage stopped in front of a stone manor house. Julian descended the carriage steps to the ground and waited patiently for Madeleine to exit. She struggled, rising from her seat, gathering her massive layers of skirt. The fabric stretched wide; she scarcely saw where to place her foot to step to the ground below.

"Come to me," Julian said; as if he knew she could not see the footrest, he reached for her satin-covered foot, his fingers gliding across her ankle. "That's it, just like that."

She felt the stair tread with her foot and motioned to step downward, sensing his hand on the hollow of her back. Distracted by his touch and unaccustomed to a heeled shoe, she slipped, falling backward.

"I have you," he breathed, catching her, swinging her into his arms. "I will not let you fall."

She nestled awkwardly in his arms, her feet dangling in the air, the side of her face too close to his mouth, to the man who had kissed her before. He leaned closer still to her hair, breathing in her scent, causing shivers to tickle her spine. She twisted in his arms, finding herself locked firmly in his embrace. Curious, she sought his hazel eyes, measuring his kindness, fretting that the truth might be discovered.

She patted his arm. "You have saved me, Captain. Protected me like a good officer would. Now, assist me to the ground."

"Such gratitude," he snickered, smiling wickedly. "If you insist, Mrs. Benoit." Slowly, Julian permitted her to slide down the length of his brawny form; she felt her face blushing red.

The manor door opened, and a robust man hurried forth. "Wedded bliss, it suits you well."

"Not yet," Jason replied, his hand hovering against her waist again, "but we propose to give married life a try. René, my wife, Mrs. Benoit."

Madeleine stepped forward and the gentleman breached the gap between them, accepting her hand with a merry grin.

"Enchanté, Mrs. Benoit," René said, his face creasing. "Julian has found himself a beautiful wife. Please, come inside. Welcome to my home."

"Thank you for hosting our wedding feast," Madeleine replied, curtseying. "Julian and I are grateful for your hospitality."

"The pleasure is mine. 'Twas the least I could do to aid in the celebration of your wedding day, since I assisted in the coming together."

He winked at Julian as if they shared a private joke. Madeleine gazed at her husband suspiciously, but followed both men inside the manor. Already the home was crowded with guests. "I don't understand, perhaps an insider's joke?"

"The commander insisted I take a bride, but that should not worry you. It was high time I settled down."

"You were made to take my hand in marriage?"

"I was encouraged to select a bride. I chose you."

"It took a bit of arm-twisting," René said, laughing loudly, then nudging Julian against his arm and leading them to the great room. "I nearly lugged the rapscallion to the altar myself to please the king, but Julian soon realized the fruit of my wisdom," he said with a wink. "Thank you for falling into his arms by the way and aiding in my ambition."

Madeleine would have commented on the tart statement, but shortly thereafter, guests surrounded her. A group of fellow daughters pulled her aside, separating her from her new husband. They spoke near the fireplace hearth, but she watched Julian with a degree of interest as he, too, was soon surrounded.

"You look beautiful," Geneviève said, smiling. "I hope I'm as lovely as you on my wedding day."

Marie blew a hair from her eyes. "It was a great deal of work on my part, but the effort is entirely worth the effect."

"I appreciate the wonders you worked on my behalf," Madeleine said, grasping Marie's wrist. "You have fashioned me into a princess. But Marie, I see the sad turn of your eye. What's wrong, my friend?"

"The separation," Geneviève responded, seeming sad herself. "You leave tomorrow with the captain. Marie misses you already."

"Is it true?"

Marie stepped closer. "What will I do without you? You're my safe harbor in this new world. I would plead for you to stay, but a woman must acquiesce to her husband's expectations."

Madeleine felt sad seeing the frown on her best friend's face. "I wish there were some way…"

"I'd have to wed one of these officers." She waved her hand as if soliciting a prospect.

"You best get busy, then. What of the boy in the corner? He keeps giving you the eye."

"Mousy. Not my type."

"He's dreamy," Geneviève purred, studying the young man.

"Perhaps you should talk to him?"

"As Sister Abby has instructed, it would not be proper for me to approach a potential suitor. Better for a man to call on a lady, like a true gentleman. So, I will wait."

"I suppose we must mind our manners," Madeleine replied, turning to Marie. "Has any gent attempted to court you, Marie?"

"No one in particular, but I was considering the doctor onboard the Saint-Jean," she said with a pout, "but that's impossible, as he's not a permanent resident of the colony. He will soon return to France."

"You've turned down a few suitors?"

"I'm waiting for the right man. I understand the reason for my arrival in New France, but I'm not chattel chained to a man like an animal. I will wait for the man who causes my heart to beat fast."

Madeleine reflected on the comment as an officer pressed into their conversation. "I could assist your heart to a faster rhythm," he jested, licking his lips. "If you would permit a meeting."

Julian came into the conversation. "Marie, allow me to introduce Gauvain."

"Enchanté, Mademoiselle." He bowed elegantly, sweeping his hand outward, causing Marie to blush.

"Nice to make your acquaintance," she mumbled, her voice tittering, her cheeks flaming a rosy hue of pink.

"Gauvain will accompany us in the morning. Should you fancy him, he's in want of a wife, is that not right, Officer?"

"I'm definitely in want," he said with a wink, rising. "Would the lady welcome a visit? Chaperoned, of course."

Julian gazed at Madeleine meaningfully. "Should the partnership be mutually acceptable to both parties, Marie would journey with us to Fort Sainte-Anne."

Madeleine watched her friend turn into a simpering ninny, completely dazzled by the young officer. Maybe Marie's curiosity grew from the offer to travel, thus not losing her friendship, or perhaps she welcomed the attention.

"I would fancy a conversation with you, Monsieur Gauvain," Marie said demurely, placing her hand on his arm. "Lead me to the refreshment table. We shall see if you can satisfy."

"My Lady, I always satisfy, but first I see to your thirst."

"If you'll excuse me," Geneviève said with a giggle, sighting the officer she had been observing before. "I'll introduce myself, after all."

"Leaves us alone," Julian said to Madeleine. "Are you hungry?"

Madeleine's tummy seemed to respond with a twinge, a

heaviness settling in the lowest part of her abdomen. She frowned, touching her belly.

"Madeleine, is something wrong?"

"I'm sure it's nothing," she retorted, placing her hand on his elbow. "I'm hungry, that's all it is. Hunger pains."

"Come to the banquet table. René has a feast of Stephen waiting and I cannot wait to dig in."

CHAPTER 15

*J*ulian saw a change in his wife's demeanor. She ate little, fingering her pigeon pie, neglecting the compote and meringues, leaving tempting morsels uneaten on her plate. Why? She had expressed her hunger earlier. Maybe the constant attention from their guests made her uncomfortable, or maybe her dress was bound too tight. Whatever the reason, her lack of conversation and obvious unease worried him.

He scrutinized her pallid expression. The color seemed to drain from her face, her forehead tensed, and rosebud lips parted in distress. "Madeleine, is something wrong?"

She drew her hand against her abdomen and held her stomach. He contemplated where her hand grasped the ivory satin gown, her fingers knotting in the fabric.

"Julian," she whispered, flushing, "I'm in pain."

"Something you ate?" he asked, stepping to her side and taking her plate.

"Perhaps the lamb was disagreeable. I do feel ill. My belly, my abdomen, it aches."

"The hour is early, but maybe we should retire for the evening? Get you home so you can rest? Shall I arrange to have the carriage brought around?"

Madeleine nodded yes.

"Mesdames et Messieurs," Julian said with a slight frown, "my wife and I must take our leave."

"No…" several officers grumbled at the same time.

"The party was just getting started," someone yelled.

"Boys, we are sorry to disappoint, but we must take our leave to begin our wedded life together. But before we go, we wish to express our gratitude to our host, for gifts received and our appreciation for your well-wishes."

"You scamp!" Gauvain hastened to say, spilling some of his drink. "Captain, are you eager?"

"Julian…" Madeleine pressed closer to his side.

"A woman this beautiful?" Julian passed Madeleine's plate into Gauvain's hands. "What husband would not be excited? Come, my bride."

He grasped Madeleine's arm and ushered her from the manor house. Standing on the front stoop, he whistled for the carriage. The guests followed them outside and formed a receiving line around them. Smiling, he made small talk until the carriage stopped where they stood. Whooping and hollering, and a general round of cheers echoed through the night as he assisted his wife inside the carriage. Once they were safely seated inside and underway, he began his inquiries.

"What's wrong? Any fool could see you're in pain."

She leaned against the seat-rest, pulling her knees to her chest.

"Madeleine, you can trust me."

She turned toward him, a sorrowful expression pinching her face, stealing the brightness from her eyes. "I cannot tell you; you will hate me…"

"Why would I have cause to hate?"

"The reason."

"What reason? Have you been keeping something from me?"

She didn't say anything for the span of several seconds. The expression on her face seemed dire, crestfallen, awash with fear. Julian worried what was coming next.

"I'm with child," she exclaimed.

Had Julian heard her correctly? She was with child? How did he respond to such a confession? He leaned against the backrest, choosing to remain silent lest he say something he would regret.

"I'm sorry! I wanted to tell you, I tried to tell you at the altar; I should have confessed the truth sooner, from the start!"

Wide-mouthed, he stared at his bride, watching tears slip from her beautiful amber eyes. *What had she said?* Had she spoken true? Expecting a baby? This must be some kind of a cruel joke, but as he watched her and saw the shock and surprise scrunch her face, he knew she had told him the truth.

"How dare you fill my heart with regret by lying to me."

"I'm sorry. Nothing I say will make a difference."

"I placed a ring on your finger, brought you into my life.

We said our vows before God and friends. Lies whispered in the most sacred of places. Damn it anyway, woman, what can I say in response to this revelation? I'm in shock, Madame."

She crumpled forward, *moaning*, and he remembered she was in pain, and now he understood why.

A baby, she was with child...

"Madeleine—" He tried to speak, swallowing the news, wanting to ask why she had not confessed the truth sooner, but the officer in him needed to take control. Needed to take care of his wife. *His wife?* Any fool could see her pain. The way he saw it, there were two choices to make and the first required his care. He pulled her into his arms. "Do you cry from the revelation, or..."

"The baby," she shrieked, sobbing, rocking in her distress. "I must be losing the baby..."

He gazed at Madeleine, taking in her suffering, worrying what might come next. He wasn't prepared for this turn of affairs, and even though he was an officer accustomed to tricky situations, he didn't know how to manage this new condition. He wanted to care, wanted to offer his compassion, but he didn't know what to say. Silence seemed to be the best option.

"Driver," Julian commanded, bellowing. "Take us to my lodgings as quickly as you can. My wife, you see, *my bride*, she is unwell. Hurry, take us home."

JULIAN STOOD BY THE HEARTH, holding a cut-glass beaker of cognac in his hands, remembering...

When they arrived at his manor house, he swooped Madeleine into his arms and carried her over the threshold. She had not protested his hold and had reached to him having no one else but her husband to trust. A clever woman to plot such a strategy, he found her as light as a feather but the weight she carried caused his heart to constrict. No wonder she had taken ill. No meat on her bones to sustain a child.

He took her directly to his bedchamber, laying her on his bed. *Not in the way he had imagined—*

Madeleine was with child; she had lied to him by keeping her condition a secret!

He sent the coachman in search of a doctor, with Madeleine pleading for the ship's surgeon, which meant the good doctor had known of her condition. *Christ's bloody nails.* The deception angered him, causing him to question her trickery. *Duped!* Forsaken by a new wife who was carrying another man's child. He paced near the hearth, anger darkening his mood further.

Drink up, Julian.

What else could he do until the ship's surgeon completed his examination? He was in agony. Frustrated, he waited for news of his wife's health. He stood near the fireplace. A log burned in the hearth, with orange and blue flames licking the timber. Holding a beaker of cognac, he gazed at the amber liquid, swirling the elixir round and round. In frustration, he gulped the spirit in one smooth swallow, soon suffering the after-burn at the base of his throat and the heat inside his mouth. The alcohol did not assuage the anger coursing through his veins, but perhaps once he partook of a few more sips, he might be calm enough to speak to his new wife.

Finally, Julian could suffer the wait no longer. Placing the glass on the mantle, he walked to his bedchamber and stood near the door.

Should he enter? Should he wait outside? *Damn this situation.* A man should not have to ponder knocking at his own damn door. Still, he rapped his knuckles against the woodgrain, striking three times.

"Come in," said Martin Lefeuve.

Julian pushed the door open and stepped inside the room. The surgeon stood near the commode, rinsing his hands in the washbasin. Julian dismissed the bloodstained water and looked at his wife who lay atop his bed covered with a thick woolen coverlet. God almighty. A fool could see her eyes were red from crying, giving voice to his fears and a pause to his anger. The bridal dress discarded, it hung on a hook on the door. He supposed she was close to naked beneath the coverlets.

It hardly mattered, he would not touch her now.

"Surgeon Martin," he said with a grimace, "we need to have a discussion."

"Perhaps it's best if we talk in the other room, Captain Benoit. Madeleine has warned me you have only just learned of her condition. And her situation is precarious."

Julian glanced at the hardwood floor, his hand clenching and unclenching at his side. "No more secrets between us, anything that needs to be disclosed, especially in terms of Madeleine's health, is best shared inside this room."

The reply was spoken to the doctor, but Julian eyed his

wife meaningfully. As if she could not bear his inquiry, maybe the implied warning too, she placed her hand against her forehead and closed her eyes.

"Madeleine," the surgeon said, expressing his concern, "is this permissible to you? As my patient, you're my primary concern. I will mind your care before I respond to a grilling from your husband."

Taking a huge breath, she drew a quivering hand through her hair, messing the soft layers that earlier had been piled high atop her head in a well-styled chignon. Now, her hair hung loose around her shoulders in wisps of disarray, highlighting her condition. Julian did not like the change.

"He's my husband," Madeleine said with a whimper. "He has every right to stand inside his own bedchamber. Every right to ask questions of you, of me."

"Hmm," the doctor said, grabbing a towel. He walked nearer to Julian, drying his hands. "I see you're upset, but be warned, Monsieur Benoit. This is a time for restraint. There's more to be considered than the circumstance you find yourself in. A mother's life, and a child's life are at stake. They are my primary concern."

"Doctor, I'm not an aggressive person," Julian said, his tone sharp. "I'll not put my wife or her child at further risk, but her health situation must be disclosed if I am to aid in her recovery."

"Can you lower your voice and control your temper?"

Julian nodded, taking a deep breath.

"As far as I can tell, your wife is approximately five, maybe six months along. She's experiencing cramping and has suffered heavy bleeding."

"Has she lost the child?"

"Not yet, but the risk of a premature birth is apparent."

Julian looked at his wife. She appeared sad and vulnerable lying in the bed. He missed her smile and the brightness of her eyes. He took a step toward her, but paused, thinking better of the approach.

"I'm sorry, Julian."

Her voice wobbled. The tears seeped from her eyes and slid along the contours of her flushed cheeks. He returned his scrutiny to the doctor. "What are the chances of saving the child?"

"Given the blood loss and continued pains, the situation seems dire. There's a good chance the child will be lost. The babe could already be dead in the womb. The mother has not sensed any recent movement."

Julian edged closer to the bed. Madeleine appeared fragile, and frightened. *How can I help her? Do I want to help her?*

"Maybe it's for the best."

Julian heard the bad tiding slip from Madeleine's mouth and wondered why a soon-to-be mother would say something so cruel.

"Look," the doctor retorted, "I'm aware you had no prior knowledge of your wife's condition when you married Mademoiselle Bourbonnais. The marriage can be annulled, whether or not she keeps the child or miscarries."

"I have considered annulling the marriage. What happens to Madeleine if I do as you suggest?"

"Madeleine would be seen as unfit to remain in New France. She would return to France when the Baptiste leaves port, which might be best as I'm leaving with the ship. I can care for her, given I understand her condition."

"And then what?"

"Why should you care what happens next; she shall no longer be a concern to you."

"Like hell!" Julian snarled, angering again. "Madeleine is not an animal to be discarded without care. She is my wife. I promised to love, honor, and cherish this woman for the rest of my life." He paused, swallowing his anger. "To accept her in sickness and in health. What kind of a man am I if I spurn her when she needs me most?"

"May I remind you," the doctor said indignantly, tossing the towel on the commode, "she carries another man's child? She lied to you. She is no better than a prostitute. Your promise did not include submitting to her lies or another man's progeny. You have every right to annul this marriage."

Madeleine gasped, pulled the covers above her head and hid beneath them.

"My wife has deceived me, yes she has, but Madeleine is not a prostitute. If any man makes such an accusation, I will hit the bastard."

"Well, you best not strike the man who recognizes the truth, for his hands are required to care for the woman lying in your bed."

"Madeleine," Julian begged, coming to the bed and searching for her fingers beneath the coverlets. "Tell me the doctor's account is not true."

"I'm not a woman of the night," she whispered sheepishly, "in this, I have told you the truth."

She peeked from beneath the covers, gazing at him

momentarily, then closed her eyes shut tight. Julian was not convinced. *Even now when the truth is known, she lies.*

"Why did you place me in this situation? What do you want from me?"

"Nothing, Julian. You don't owe me anything. I have deceived you. 'Tis like the doctor said, I should return to France."

He knelt on the floor beside the bed. "But you tried to tell me the truth at the altar. Am I right?"

Madeleine nodded. She could not speak or did not want to. She whimpered, groaning, her beautiful face contorting in pain. He reached for her hand and held on tight.

"Madeleine," Julian said, sighing, pulling her into his arms. "It will be all right."

She earnestly began to wail.

"Doctor, this situation is urgent. How do I help my wife? What do I do?"

"You don't have to call her that."

"Look, we are man and wife. We have said our vows before God and my wife is in pain. You're a doctor, you smarmy bastard, help her!"

"I have done all I can. Time must take its course."

"Is there anything, anything that can be done to save the child?"

"No one has a crystal ball, but it might help if Madeleine were calmer. Complete bed rest, maybe warm compresses on her belly. Tea, and a husband's support."

"Madeleine and I are supposed to leave the city tomorrow morning. I have my orders to depart."

"You would take me?" Madeleine asked.

"If she has not aborted the baby by morning, there is a chance she might carry the child to term, but I must impress on you the importance of rest. Madeleine must have complete bed rest. She must not travel. The jostling would not serve her situation well."

"I understand. I will ask you to leave us now."

"There is one more action that might assist."

"Of course, anything."

"Mademoiselle Marie is aware of your wife's condition. Her friendship might be a comfort."

"I shall arrange for her to come in the morning," Julian said, unsurprised Marie was involved in this conspiracy.

"I will stay the night to care for my patient."

"You will have to sleep on the floor but there's a bedroll and blankets in the small room. You understand why I cannot fetch them."

"I can tend to my own needs," Doctor Martin said, walking to the door. "I leave you now, to talk to your wife."

After the surgeon left and they were alone in the bedchamber, Julian leaned forward and grasped Madeleine's hand. She stared at him. "How did I find a man such as you?"

"A pushover, you mean? This attention does not mean anything. For all intents and purposes, we're still strangers who have only just met. Who knows what the future holds, but what God has put together, no man shall put asunder, not even your husband."

"What? You cannot possibly mean what you say. No man has ever shown me such understanding."

He crawled under the coverlets, lying beside his wife, and pulled her semi-naked figure into his embrace. "Save your energy. Try to remain calm and not worry overly. For the unborn child, you understand."

Puffing a sigh, she nodded, placing her head on his shoulder. "Will you stay with me? I'm frightened of being alone."

"I will not leave you. Try to get some rest."

EXHAUSTED, Julian slipped from the bed covers once Madeleine had fallen asleep. He crossed the floor to the fireplace, adding another log to the fire, wanting to keep the bedchamber warm and comfortable. Sparks flew from the fire and the flames licked at the bark. He watched the orange hues dancing, contemplating how he had come to this place. He turned to the bed to contemplate his sleeping wife.

Quiet now, the pains had stopped. Madeleine had not passed the child. She was still expecting. For her sake and the life of her baby, he must put his personal feelings aside, at least until the danger was past. How long must he wait? How long must he hold his grief inside? He wanted to rage aloud! Scream injustice. But, shouting at his wife might result in further heartache, and he would not be held responsible for the death of a child.

Julian realized he had had the opportunity to learn the truth earlier, when his wife paused at the altar, delaying the acceptance of her vows. The pondering had been odd, but he had ignored his own good sense.

Decisions must be made now. Did he want to annul the marriage? He probably should. But studying his wife, breathing easy, sleeping peacefully in his bed, annulment did not seem the right course of action.

Hours had passed. Bone-tired, Julian returned to the bed. He removed his lawn shirt and breeches and threw them on an armchair. He climbed beneath the coverlets. Turning away from his wife, he punched the pillow and succumbed to sleep.

CHAPTER 16

When Madeleine awoke, she lay on her left side, nestled in the downy cotton of Julian's straw bed. She recognized her labor pains had ended, *to her relief,* but the knowledge her baby might be safe was not what caused her to open her eyes in surprise.

Julian's warm body cuddled close to her, his breath exhaling against her neck, causing tiny ripples of awareness. His pelvis pressed against her bottom, his arm was slung leisurely across her waist, and his hand dangling near her rounded belly. She took a deep inhalation of air, not daring to move.

He's naked... he wouldn't dare? Would he?

But Julian rolled to his back. Madeleine sighed, relieved the contact had ended, rolling to her back as well and soon staring at the wood-planked ceiling. A fluttering of motion; a life stirred inside her belly. She sighed. *The baby was alive.* Was she glad?

Julian awoke, rubbed his eyes, then turned to his wife. Not saying anything, she scrutinized his expression, seeing the uncertainty in his hazel eyes, wondering what he was thinking. She looked at him, studying the smooth contour of his chest.

"How are you feeling this morning?" he asked, concern written in the gray hollows beneath his hazel eyes. She could tell he had not slept much.

"I'm scared to move. Frightened the pains will begin again."

"Understandable after your suffering."

"But other needs are pressing."

"Use the privy," he said with some seriousness, staring fixedly at her. "And then get back in bed."

She raised her eyebrows. "You sound like an officer, commanding your men."

"I am an officer, and whether I like it or not, you're in my charge."

She glanced at him, grasped the blankets but did not speak.

"A chair and a chamber pot are behind the screen. Do you need my help?"

"I can find my way."

Madeleine climbed slowly from the bed, wearing only a white linen shirt that barely covered her buttocks. It did not belong to her and as she walked across the floor, she saw the way Julian reacted to this, his surprise, watching her retreat wearing one of his shirts. She hid behind the screen, attended to her ablutions, then returned to her husband's bed.

"Has the bleeding stopped?" he asked, not touching her, seeming to accept the situation.

"It appears so." She felt the baby move again; she paused where she was standing, placing her hand on her rounded belly. He watched, seeing the truth's evidence.

"What is it?" Julian asked, throwing the covers aside. Leaving the bed, he rushed to her side. "More pain?"

"No, no pain. 'Tis only, the baby moved."

"A good sign," he said, his expression sullen. "Now back to bed as the doctor told us this was best."

Julian clutched her arm. Madeleine gazed at him, his warm fingers against her arm, permitting him to escort her across the small space while contemplating his nakedness. Uncomfortable, she glanced away, but not before he noticed her insecurity.

"Do my attributes make you uncomfortable?"

"No." She swallowed, lying.

He assisted her to lie down, sheltering her beneath the coverlets. Grasping his shirt, Julian put it on, seeing through her falsehoods. "It's best you become comfortable."

She leaned against the pillows, trying to relax. "Because you'll continue to be my husband? And take your liberties, after everything you have learned?"

"There's much we could say on the subject, but I won't upset you."

He slid his fingers through his hair; he walked to an armchair close to where she lay and took a seat.

"I'm sorry, Julian."

"Madeleine, look, I will not say or do anything that will

harm you or your unborn child, but this situation comes as a shock. Why would you travel to the colony, expecting no less, to marry the first chump who greeted you?"

"I was not looking for a patsy. I required a husband."

"For yourself, or for your child?"

"For both of us."

"You're at least five months with child," he said with a frown, pulling the covers from her belly. "You could not have hidden this—this bump—much longer."

The baby moved, and she saw Julian watching her belly bulge. He sighed, but did not shy away from his curiosity. She permitted him to pull the shift higher, sliding the shirt edge to expose her creamy skin. Closing her eyes, she shivered while his fingers drifted across her skin, initiating a tingling awareness, soon splaying his hand against her belly.

"Wow," he said with a degree of fascination. "The little one feels like a fish darting to the surface."

"Does it upset you, to touch me?"

"It upsets me you're with child," he said, frowning, removing his hand. "This is not the way I wanted my life, my marriage, to begin. This child will not be mine."

"It could be yours. Girl or boy, it could call you Father."

"Do not look at me as if I'm some sort of prince charming who will save you from past mistakes. I'm a captain with a company to command, an officer, nothing more. It would please you, wouldn't it, if I supported your grand scheme?"

"A part of me," she admitted, losing a tear, "wishes the baby had died inside my womb. It would serve our purposes to start a life together, but it's not the child's fault the father forced himself on me. I have tried to come to terms with this situation."

"I understand your feelings, and sympathize with the circumstances that brought you here, but don't wish ill on your child, Madeleine. It's not the motherly thing to do."

"Sooner or later, you will not want me," she said, shaking her head. "This child will always come between us."

The baby moved again. "Did you see it move?" he said with surprise. "It's probably a boy. I should wake the doctor and have him examine you."

"If you desire it. What about travel today?"

"In a few days. I don't want to put this little fellow or his mother at risk."

"You think it's a boy?"

"Certain of it," Julian replied, sliding her shirt down and covering her with the sheets. "This child's a fighter, just like his mother."

"You think I'm a fighter?"

"Most women would not brave the Atlantic Ocean in the best of circumstances, simply to find a husband."

"Is that what I've found?" she asked, her brows rising with the question. Her teeth grasping her lip, hoping.

"It's too soon to speak of commitment. I need to dress, talk to my commander, to René, inform him of our change in plans." He turned to her. "I'll see to your care. That's all I can promise."

"I understand."

"I will send for Marie and have her sit with you."

"I would like that."

Madeleine watched him dress, taking in his virility, his

masculinity, seeing he was not shy. There must have been other women. Once Julian was dressed, he brought the surgeon into the bedchamber. Departing soon after, he left them alone.

She permitted Doctor Martin's medical inspection again.

CHAPTER 17

"Madeleine is with child," Julian said, seated in front of his commander's desk. "For the first time in my life, I have no idea what to do. I'm caught in a trap."

"This news comes as a surprise," René replied, leaning backward on his chair, throwing his quill on the desk. "How dare the chit take advantage of an officer. As far as I'm concerned, there's only one course of action. Annul the marriage. Send her back to France on the return voyage of Le Baptiste."

"Merde," Julian grumbled, taking a deep breath, sliding his hand through his hair. "Most men in my position would do as you suggest, but confound me, my ass is in the air. If I do as you say, there's a risk, not only to the unborn child but also to the mother. She has me by the balls."

"For foutre sake, calm yourself, you're hardly the father and the way I see it, you're not responsible for her care. Once she's onboard the ship, her welfare is no longer your concern."

"You don't understand, I must negotiate this situation carefully. Madeleine took sickly during the reception. She started to bleed. If I upset her further, I could threaten the child. By some miracle, she still carries this morning."

"A convenient truth if you ask me. Look, get your head out of your arse; her dilemma is none of your concern. It's good of you to offer your support, officers are charged to serve and protect, but this mess is not your responsibility. Let it go. Annul the marriage on the grounds that she's a woman of middling nature."

"Seems cruel to push her aside and force her back onboard the ship. Surely it's my responsibility to care for my wife? I have taken Madeleine Bourbonnais before God and his witnesses, to have and to hold…"

"Who are you trying to convince? God would not see you saddled with another man's responsibility."

"I must consider both sides. Would a good, kind, and loving God expect me to have mercy? What will happen to Madeleine if I do as you say? Could she survive the return voyage to France? At her arrival to this country, she was frail."

"I'm sorry I put you in this position. This is my fault."

"You did force me to marry."

"'Tis true enough, but you chose the bride. Is it worse? Is she a prostitute, a fille de joie?"

"I hardly think so. She claims she was forced into an unpleasant situation to satisfy her father's gambling debts. The child is the product of a rape."

René shook his head. "A terrible circumstance if it's true. Do you believe her?"

"What should I believe?" Julian raised his hands in

exasperation. "The facts as they present include an expectant wife. Damn it, I didn't anticipate this complication."

"Annul the marriage, send her back to France and choose another woman."

"But what will happen to Madeleine and her child if I do as you suggest?"

"She will probably be sent to an asylum for unwed mothers, for women unfit to have a husband."

Julian cringed, imagining Madeleine locked away, *again*, in the Hôpital Général. "No one deserved such a fate. Lock her up? Send Madeleine to the asylum she escaped from, that's a horrible solution to my problem. I will not do it."

René shook his head, chuckling, his cheeks reddening with the humor. "She really does have you by the balls. If you care so much for your *new wife*," he said with a smirk, slapping his knee, "keep the marriage. Work it out. Eventually, you were bound to be a father. Your child or someone else's, what does it matter? All children born in this colony will please the king."

"I need to weigh the pros and cons, but if I remain in the marriage, I cannot leave for Fort Sainte-Anne until Madeleine is fit to travel. It could be days."

"A few days will not matter," René exclaimed, studying Julian intently. "Tell me true, Captain Benoit, do you fancy the woman, despite the child?"

Grief-stricken, Julian considered the question. Until the news, he had been eager to build a life with Madeleine, excited to pursue an emotional and physical bond. If he put aside his issues with the child, he realized that his feelings toward the mother had not changed. But now he was forced to consider two people and having to care for them both.

"I was attracted to Madeleine from the start." Julian sighed, recalling their first introductions at the harbor on the morning of the galleon's arrival. "Though the addition has not altered my good opinion of the woman. Most men finding themselves in my circumstances would walk away, rejecting the setup, but when I look at her eyes…"

"You're conflicted, what man wouldn't be? However, there's no shame in loving the woman, Julian. No shame in loving the child either for that matter."

"From what you say, one might think the decision was straightforward, easy even."

"Well, sometimes we let our ego get in the way. If you care for Madeleine, and personally I think you do, then no one can fault you for remaining true to your vows. Can you live with the future and what it might bring?"

"How should I know? The ship's surgeon has pointed out to me, only time will tell."

"Then give it time and don't make a rash decision."

MADELEINE BEGAN to cry as soon as Marie opened the door to the bedchamber. A friendly face and she dearly needed to see one. She had fallen further by deceiving a good man and feared she would never have a better life.

"Oh my," Marie exclaimed, closing the door and hurrying to the bed where she lay. "What's wrong? Has your husband forced himself on you? Has he hurt you?"

"No—" Madeleine sniveled, the tears spilling from her eyes. "It's nothing like that."

"I knew something was not right when Julian asked me to visit, but he kept his confidence to himself. Can you tell me, what's happened?"

What had happened? Madeleine suffered from acute numbness, knowing she had made the worst mistake of her life. "Did he not tell you?"

"He has not confided anything. Madeleine, why are you upset?" Marie sat beside her on the edge of the bed, waiting for a reply. "You can tell me."

"It's the baby."

"What about the baby?"

"My pains began last night. I started to bleed during the reception. I was forced to tell Julian the truth. On our wedding night, *our wedding night*, that I was with child."

"Oh dear," Marie said with some seriousness. "I don't know what to ask of you first, your husband's response to your confession, or if you still carry."

"The baby is safe," Madeleine wailed, choking on her words, thumping the bed with her hand. "But as you can imagine, my new husband is angry, and terribly upset."

"I feel the need to lie down." Marie groaned, removing her bonnet from her head and laying it on the commode beside the basin. "This is a turn of events, though I see you're still in his bed. I suppose it's positive that he has not asked you to leave his house. Move over, Maddie, make a space for me."

Madeleine edged to the right and Marie climbed onto the

bed, stretching, laying her head on the pillow. Marie had a point, Julian had not discarded her, not yet.

"What now? What do you think will happen?"

"The ship's surgeon has suggested annulling the marriage, sending me back to France. I cannot go there. They'll put me in the…"

"That horrible hospital the night watchman fetched you from," Marie said with a gasp, glancing at her meaningfully. "Would the captain stoop so low?"

"I don't know what he'll do."

"Madeleine, your husband's frustration shouldn't come as a surprise. It must have been a shock learning the truth. Most men would struggle with the knowledge that their wife was expecting another man's child."

"I understand his frustration," Madeleine said, turning to her side to contemplate Marie. "But this is a new world, a new land where ideas and opportunity abound. He might give me a second chance?"

A second chance, even as Madeleine said the words, she knew her prospects were dimming like the setting sun. Marie's grimace, her melancholy expression, satisfied her question, squashing her hopes. Julian would cast her from his life.

"'Tis a new world, yes," Marie said, nibbling at her lip, "though certainly not a place where new opinions of understanding will aid your position. Let me assure you, church theology will not extend to matters of immodesty. We live in a world where church, state, and a gentleman's code are tightly interwoven. Women seldom earn mercy and must submit to the position."

"Marie, your worldly view depresses me. I thought you were my friend."

"A loyal friend does not offer hope where hope cannot be found. It will not serve you to see the good captain like a bouquet of roses held in a woman's hands. Life does not smell so sweet. That time is over, I'm afraid. Should the captain declare he doesn't want you, you'll have to find your way on your own or be subject to whatever outcome he chooses."

It sounded so dire. Madeleine didn't want to be left alone to her own decision-making skills, neither did she want her fate determined by her husband. What was she to do? She yearned for someone to watch over her, to take care of her, love her. She recalled the expression on Julian's face, the shock at the news, the hurt laid at his feet. She couldn't escape from his rejection, her future seemed dire.

"That's impossible. A woman could never exist in this new world without a husband."

"Why not?" Marie exclaimed. "You managed well enough until the night watchman captured you from the street."

"Yes, well, what I learned while living as an orphan is that I don't want to return to such a vocation. And this Ville de Québec, it's ruthless, wild and rugged. How could I ever manage on my own? I, we, could be captured by native warriors."

"Now you're talking nonsense. They're people, Madeleine. There's nothing unseemly about that in my estimation."

"But I have heard some are dangerous, hiding in the forest, lurking, waiting to catch you unaware."

"Tales told at night to frighten young children. True

enough, dangers are found in the dark of night, no matter where one lives, I might add, but I have witnessed the native people trading their furs. I understand some officers in want of a wife have gone so far as to wed aboriginal women. Perhaps the opposite approach could be a possibility."

"Marrying an aboriginal man?" Madeleine said with surprise, rising on the bed. "That's not something I would have considered."

"I wouldn't object to the possibility." Marie winked, licking her lips. "A man is a man after all, but each to their own. What of your child, if your husband rejects you?"

"The baby will come into the world regardless," Madeleine said, scrutinizing Marie. "What of Gauvain? What do you think of him?"

"He's a player. A wolf," Marie said, shaking her head, gazing at her with bright eyes. "A handsome brute, nonetheless, but fortunately for me, there are few women who can capture his attention in this colony. Regardless, I'm confident I have made an impression."

Madeleine's fingers played with the blankets. "You did speak of aboriginal maidens. Would they strike his fancy?"

"Silly Maddie, not even our other sisters, the king's daughters, could hold a candle to me."

"You will have a meeting with Gauvain?"

"Maybe," Marie mumbled, sighing. "I find him attractive. But something else pleases me more in regard to a possible match."

"What would that be?"

"Gauvain will travel to Fort Sainte-Anne with your

husband. If Julian doesn't cast you aside, and he would be a fool to do so by the way, a match with Gauvain means you and I could remain together. I will not lose my friend. I will do what I must to settle in the same place."

"You would choose a man that might not be faithful to you? Marry to be where I am?"

"If he takes me. Gauvain has not requested a meeting of introduction. However, it's early days. I only made his acquaintance yesterday eve."

"Marie, that would be perfect, to settle in the same place."

"I think so."

"There will be dangers. Julian has told me the officers are settling along the river to protect the colony from Iroquois warriors, perhaps a British invasion, too."

"Maybe it would be better for us to return to France," Marie retorted, giggling.

"I hardly relish another passing on the Atlantic Ocean," Madeleine groaned, recalling her sickness. "The first voyage nearly did me in, so I must take my chances here."

"You must state your case and beg mercy of your husband to keep your marriage. It's unlikely Julian has experienced intimacy in some time; it couldn't hurt to…"

The thought of human contact caused Madeleine's heart to constrict, her anxiety levels to rise. She didn't want such an overture of carnal abuse ever again.

"No," Madeleine asserted, her brow wrinkling, "I cannot give him anything of an intimate nature. The baby…"

"I don't want to play devil's advocate, Maddie, but maybe it would be better if the baby came early."

"Despite how this child was conceived, I could not live with such an outcome."

Marie grasped her chin, compelling her to look in her direction. "I'm certain Captain Benoit will not shirk his duties, despite the difficulty. He will come to see he's right to stand by his wife if you give him reason to care."

"How can you be so certain?"

"Look in the mirror for your answer. See for yourself."

Madeleine smiled despite her worries. "Are you saying I'm a catch?"

"You were the beauty on the boat, not I. The woman who drew the crew's attention on the ship when they should have been tending to their duties, scrubbing the deck, watching for land, or some other odd dangers. Julian Benoit would be a fool to part with such a prize."

"Even if the prize comes with an extra mouth to feed?"

"Even so," Marie said, smiling. "I predict the captain will keep his new wife."

It was kind of Marie to share her optimism, attempting to rebuild her self-esteem, but why would any man accept such responsibility? She couldn't see it happening.

"Sounds well and good, but why would Julian take such a risk?"

"Because at the root of it, the captain is a good and responsible man who takes his role seriously. Though I think there's something else, a basic human need that he is missing, that you can fill, Madeleine."

"I wish I could see this trouble through your eyes. Despite everything, my husband has been kind."

"Madeleine, regardless that you could lose your child, when you're better, you must encourage a future with, um, your husband."

"What do you suggest?"

"Consummate your marriage. Give your husband the bare necessity he's been missing. Your future depends on gaining his attention."

Madeleine considered the child growing inside her womb. She had to keep the baby safe, but to keep her marriage safe, did she have to beg the affection of her husband? She wasn't sure she could do it. Gambling on her future? Lying with a man, *intimately*, filled her with revulsion.

"I don't know if I can."

"He's your husband," Marie quipped, "not some reprobate who will force himself on you."

Madeleine knew she must overcome past hurtful emotions, sensations forced on her by the misdeeds of other men. Julian held himself to higher standards and carried a different moral fiber.

"He's not a rake, Madeleine, he's your husband. An officer in the king's command, born to fight. If you're to stand a chance, you must fight, too, for what you want, for the man you crossed an ocean to find."

"I'll try."

"Show some spirit, girl. You've known hunger. What do you hunger for now?"

"A future," Madeleine wailed, turning her back, shaking her head. "But it's difficult to have a positive vision of my future right now."

Marie grasped her hand. "Don't give up."

Madeleine glanced at Marie, seeing her determined expression. She'd never known anyone with such spirit. "Oh, very well, I won't give in."

"Good," Marie said, sighing. "Now, let's talk about something else."

CHAPTER 18

Madeleine heard a sound. The front door opened and closed. She heard voices. A woman. A man. *Julian.* She calmed, sucking in a shuttering breath of air. It wasn't much longer before the bedchamber door opened, and her husband of only a few hours stepped inside the room. She peeked from beneath the covers, not liking the stern expression on his face.

"You're awake."

"Yes. Just."

"We need to talk."

Madeleine nodded, watching her husband. He placed his hands on his hips.

"I have had some time to consider our situation," he confided, glancing at her, staring at the flooring. "I've considered annulling the marriage, but something gives me pause."

"I know what you're about to say. I expected consequences."

He raised his observation, staring, scrutinizing her, making her uncomfortable. "You can read my mind, then?"

"Julian," Madeleine said with a gasp, "please don't make this situation any more difficult than it already is. Pass your judgment." She paused, breathing to remain calm. "I expect you will wash your hands of me."

"I want to. I don't deny it. But I will not satisfy your conscience with anything less than the truth. You have put me in a terrible position."

"I understand."

"Do you?" he said with a grimace, moving closer. "I don't know what course of action to pursue. If I force you to return to France, what will become of you and your unborn child? I'm not unkind, nor am I unfeeling. I understand the situation, even your motivation. A woman expecting, alone, having no family and few friends to assist. I appreciate why one might seek a male victim, still…"

"I will survive. I have in the past."

"You think I'll let you go without consideration for your safety? You're my wife, my responsibility. How will you face a second journey at sea? I remember your condition after you left the boat on arrival. Weak and frail from the journey across the Atlantic, you fell into my arms."

"I was grateful for your assistance," Madeleine said with a sigh, "grateful you caught me."

He stepped closer, his expression firm. "Caught me in a trap. How could you?"

He shook his head. Madeleine studied his earnest expression, seeing how her plan had hurt him, cost him. She was guilty of deception. She placed her quivering hand on her forehead, her face flaming red, then took a deep breath and perused him directly. She didn't like conflict in her life, but situations must be faced, no matter how difficult.

"I know it's too late to say I'm sorry. I see your pain and the burden I have given you. I should not have come to this new world, thinking a man might be the answer to my problems."

"Amen to that."

"Julian Benoit, I give you permission to let me go, to release me from our contract. 'Tis only right we annul the marriage."

"Is that what you want?"

"No. Of course not."

"Then why do you suggest it?"

"I betrayed you; I need to set this right. My honesty was lacking at the altar, I didn't have the courage to face the consequences. You would have spurned me. I give you free will to take action against me, now."

"What will happen if I agree?"

Madeleine sighed, took a deep inhalation of air. "No one can divine the future. Who can know what will happen?"

"Madeleine," Julian said, striding forward, taking the armchair beside the bed. "Do you want to stay?"

She stared at his stunning hazel eyes, seeing a strength of will, an anchor she wanted to grasp with both hands and with all her strength, if only to safeguard her confidence. Many women would want him, would love him. Did she? He was a reasonable man and a handsome one, too.

"Madeleine?"

Marie had told her to fight for what she desired. She needed to try. "I do," she confided. "I do want to stay."

"Why? I must know the reason before I make a decision, either way."

"Will you believe me?"

"Do I have any other choice?"

Madeleine shifted on the bed, pulled back the covers and slid her feet over the edge. The wood floor was cold beneath her feet, but she hardly noticed. She reached across the space and took hold of Julian's hand. It was warm. He didn't speak as she gazed at him.

"Julian," Madeleine said, squeezing his hand, "you're a good man. I could love you."

He glanced away, but she managed to keep hold of his hand. "That's nice, your statement sounds nice, too. I've been waiting for such a love for most of my young life. I hoped she would come, have the courage to journey across the ocean to be with me, I just didn't…"

"Expect that a wife would arrive on these French shores holding such a high price."

He placed his free hand on top of hers. "I cannot send you back."

"Your reasoning?"

"I will not see you hurt, nor will I be held responsible for what could happen to you, or your child, if you were to sail to France."

"Of course," Madeleine replied, releasing his hand. "Captain, where do we stand then, together?"

"We are husband and wife. I will keep the promises I

made to you at the altar, but I will not consummate this marriage."

"How should I reply to such a statement?" Madeleine gasped, willing herself not to cry. "Thank you?"

"Your safety and well-being, that's all I propose."

"A marriage of convenience, then?"

"Yes. We begin on equal footing. You shall be well cared for, a roof over your head, food in your belly. You know what to expect from me, your husband, the one you sought, and I know what to expect from you."

Madeleine watched Julian rise from the armchair and retreat the way he had come, returning to the bedchamber door. She wanted to tell him she could be kind, generous and worthy of his commitment, *worthy of his love*, too, but fear held her heart in peril. He grasped the handle, turning away.

"A local woman is cooking our dinner. I will bring you a plate when it's ready."

She nodded, willing the tears not to fall. He left her then. Alone.

It struck her… *What did he expect from her?* He had not said.

CHAPTER 19

"You're past the worst," Martin Lefeuve, the ship's surgeon confided, drying his hands on a scrap of cloth. "You're certain the bleeding has stopped?"

"Yes," Madeleine replied, still abed after the doctor's examination. "I have had no further labor pains or spotting."

"That's a good sign," he said, turning to face her. "Still, it's best you restrict physical activity, not enduring too much exercise."

"I have not had the opportunity to do much of anything other than lie in this bed. Julian has not permitted me to leave the bedchamber. Must I remain abed, Doctor Martin? I would like to at least breathe fresh air."

"Minor exercise can be pursued, but nothing of a vigorous nature. I'm not sure why your labor pains began, or why you bled, but I don't want to see poor health return."

"Is there any chance the pains, the bleeding, could return?"

"Every chance, but there's also the possibility you will

progress normally with no further trouble. I would not worry until there's reason for concern."

"But I am concerned. 'Tis unnatural to bleed while carrying."

"Though many women do." The surgeon stood before her, appearing grave. "Madeleine, there's something I have not told you."

"About what?"

"Your health."

Whatever information Doc Martin had kept from her, Madeleine saw that the mystery bothered him. His brows drew together severely, and his forehead furrowed with wrinkles. It gave her cause for concern. "Will you tell me what's wrong? By the way you're staring at me, something is not right."

He walked to the bedchamber entrance and peered beyond its threshold to ensure they were alone. Shutting the door, he came to where she lay on the bed and sat on the armchair. "It's not what it seems," he said, gesturing with his hand. "I want to assure you; your health is restored."

"Why the cloak and dagger? You shut the door."

"It's a matter of respecting your privacy and ensuring that what I disclose is not heard by anyone else. Madeleine, you're fine. The baby is fine, too."

"Okay. Why are you so certain? You yourself said you could not predict the future."

He gazed at the door again. "I may have exaggerated your situation."

"What? How so? Please explain."

"You were never in any danger of losing this child. Or at

least, this is my belief."

Madeleine considered this news, remembering her labor pains. "But I was bleeding."

"True enough. But the bleeding was mild. It could have happened for any number of reasons."

Madeleine crossed her arms. "You led me to believe I might lose the child." She huffed, blowing her hair from her face. "What type of doctor would do such a thing? Put a woman through such worry."

"I have been asking myself this question for days. *Why would I do such a thing?* Lying in relation to your physical health is an ethical violation, it goes against my professional beliefs."

"Then why did you do it?"

"Your husband had learned you were in the family way, and I could see your marriage was in jeopardy. You required time to set things right. If they could be set right."

"With my husband?"

"You're a bright woman. After your personal trials, you understand what I have done for you."

"But on the ship… You said my secret should be told? My husband deserved the truth?" Madeleine shook her head, not believing what she was hearing. "Doctor Martin, have you changed your mind?"

"I want to see you happily settled. You need time to form a relationship, a bond. You're a good woman. He's a good man."

"Kind of you to say, but I'm shocked. In my experience, men do not act in such a well-meaning way unless they want something in return. What do you want from me?"

"Please, none of that nonsense. My job is to heal a patient's wounds. The ones you can see, and more often than not, the hurts that remain hidden. I take my pleasure from knowing the risk is worth the reward."

"I owe you my thanks."

"You're welcome."

"But you leave me in a state of unrest, not knowing my health condition. Is there further advice, anything I should avoid?"

He raised his brows in a speculative fashion, contemplating. "I would not recommend marital relations. Not yet. Just in case."

Madeleine lowered her head. "No worry on that accord. My husband has not achieved his marital rights. I imagine an expectant woman is not an enticement to certain pleasures."

Doctor Martin gazed at her, assessing her belly, shaking his head. "You're a beautiful woman, even with the extra weight. Still, your husband's discomfort is understandable, given the circumstances. Has he overcome the shock of learning the truth?"

"I could not tell you. He's hardly visited his wife, choosing to pursue his work as an officer, whatever work that might be. I have only talked to the hired help, and Marie. She visits me every afternoon."

"She will not come today."

"Oh, why? What news do you have of her?"

"By the look on your face, Julian has not told you. I'm surprised Marie did not share her confidence, especially with you being her closest ally and friend."

"Doc Lefeuve, I'm not a fool. You're keeping something from me. What's going on?"

A knock sounded on the door. Julian stepped inside the bedchamber.

"Marie is getting married this afternoon."

Madeleine looked between the two men, seeing an unspoken look pass between them. Why had they kept this from her? The dishonesty made her angry. She rose slowly from the bed. "I will get dressed. I must attend the wedding."

"No," Julian said, coming nearer to the bed. "I don't think that would be wise."

"You cannot stop me. I have my own free will and I plan to exercise it."

"At the risk of your unborn child?"

Madeleine gazed at the only other man in the room, hoping. "Doctor…"

"I'm sorry, Madeleine, but I must agree with your husband. Venturing outside to breathe fresh air is one thing, but attending Marie's wedding where you could greet uncertain stressors is not a good idea."

"Not fair," she pouted, sighing, sitting in resignation. "Marie has been my only support, my only friend. It distresses me she will stand at the altar alone, without the benefit of her family, or a good friend."

"Life is not always fair," Julian said, his stern expression never changing. "I have learned this thanks to you, Madame."

"'Tis not the same issue, Monsieur. Please. Do me one act of kindness."

"At the risk of your child? Is this a risk you want to take?"

Her eyes filled with fluid, she gazed at her heavy belly. "I want no harm to come to my baby, and well you know it, too."

Julian stepped forward. "I have news that should brighten your mood."

"And what is that, Monsieur?"

"Stop with the name calling. We're man and wife. It's my responsibility to care for you, no matter what. You'll submit to my guidance."

"I'll submit to my own conscience. I will stand beside my friend as she has stood beside me."

"And if the worst comes?"

Madeleine nibbled at her lip, took a deep inhalation of air. "This is my burden to carry, Julian. I will bear it as best I can, but I will not be bullied into remaining in this bed one minute longer."

"No one has a guarantee."

"Julian," Madeleine sighed, exasperated. "Please..."

"Does it mean that much to you?"

"It does."

Julian threw up his hands in exasperation. "Fine. Who am I to keep a woman from her friend."

"What were you going to say before?"

"Only that Marie has chosen to wed Gauvain."

"Gauvain," Madeleine said with some surprise. "Does this mean what I think?"

"It means you will continue your friendship when we depart Ville de Québec. You should thank your husband for making it possible."

"They're bound for Fort Richelieu?"

"As are we. You'll have your wish to leave your bed. At first light tomorrow morning."

JULIAN'S BOTTOM ached from sitting on the rigid wooden pew, but he managed the discomfort. Irritation could be mitigated with the right treatment. A man's burdens, the life decisions that came with struggle, required more patience. He tried to ignore his relationship with Madeleine, sought to focus on the bride and groom. Gauvain and Marie spoke their vows to each other, while he sat beside his wife.

'I do, and with this ring' echoed through the sanctuary.

He glanced at Madeleine, seeing the serene expression on her face. What was she thinking? What should he say to her? No words. He felt cheated and could not get past the hurt, the lie. He glanced at the couple, watching as Gauvain said his own 'I do'.

Had his colleague made the same mistake?

Julian remembered standing at the altar, speaking vows to his wife, to Madeleine. He closed his eyes, *remembering the moment*, envisioning her beauty, her perfectly coifed hair, and her wedding dress that had fit her so well. He sighed at the remembrance, not knowing then that his wife was expecting. Now, the realization caused his heart to constrict.

After the ceremony, they said their congratulations and left the chapel for their lodgings. Madeleine sat in an armchair by the hearth in the great room. She was beautiful and Julian could not help staring at her face.

"She was beautiful," Madeleine said, breaking the silence,

sighing. "Marie seemed pensive, perhaps sad. Did you notice she did not smile, not even once? Do you think the marriage was a mistake? Or maybe happiness can be found with her groom, with Gauvain?"

Julian sat in the opposite armchair. "No one can foresee the future or what the future might bring. Maybe they will be well-suited for each other, or maybe not."

"Julian, what of our relationship? Do we stand a chance at happiness?"

"I said I would support you, but please, Madeleine. Do not expect more than I can give."

"But the discomfort, this wedge between us. We cannot breach the hurt without conversation. Julian," she winced, her face crumpling, "we need to talk. Confide our opinions. Dignify our commitment by sharing time together. And... you keep to yourself," she said with a frown, glancing downward, "understandably."

"I'm trying, trying to come to terms with this situation."

"I understand, an adjustment period. But... many days have passed since we became man and wife, and you learned of my secret."

"Yes, well, one of us is ready for the conversation. Have we talked enough? I'm tired. We should retire for the night. No need to speak of unpleasant business."

"Will you sleep with me?" Madeleine nibbled at her lip, worrying.

"You're a beautiful woman but I won't touch you."

"Kind of you to say, too," Madeleine said with a sigh, standing, rubbing her aching back. "But it's your right as my husband to take your liberties, and..."

"You think I want to?"

She seemed shocked by his reply. Embarrassed by his comment, Madeleine glanced away. "Most men would take up their sex with their wife." She turned, facing him. "Still, I understand your hesitation, your lack of desire. Even why you find me inadequate."

Inadequate? She was wrong on that account. What kept him from their bed? My God, how he wanted to plant himself between their sheets, desiring to breach the distance keeping them apart. Pride. Hideous pride seized him, but he would not confess this to his wife.

"I will not beg for you to touch me. The ship's surgeon has advised me that we should avoid consummating our marriage. For now."

"I'm uncomfortable with this conversation, Madeleine."

"I went to a difficult place. Can you help me, a little? I'm responsible for this situation. I'm sorry for my part, but what can I do to make it better? I'm tired. I think I will lie down. Good night, Julian. Mine husband!"

She made to rise, stood staring at him. He didn't move, choosing to sit on the armchair like a stubborn fool. What did she expect him to say?

"Husband. You say the word as if it means something to you."

"Julian... It wasn't easy getting onboard the ship at Dieppe's grand quay. The ten weeks at sea nearly killed me. But I climbed onboard that boat, believing I needed a husband. Now that I have one, I wonder why I needed a man so badly. What has it gained me?"

Madeleine retreated from the great room, hurrying to

their bedchamber. He followed her across the threshold. "Muscle," he said with a grimace, rising to anger. "A man to take care of your every whim. That is what every woman wants, yes?"

"I did want for the care. For attention, for vows we shared together."

She retreated inside the bedchamber and seemed surprised when he followed her inside the room. He watched her remove her bonnet and place it on the commode. "Mademoiselle, do you want something from your husband?"

She turned to look at him, her lips forming the shape of an 'o'. He glimpsed the frustration in her eyes. "What could I want that you would give me? This is not a love match."

"Do you want for love?" he asked, stepping nearer.

"Every woman desires love, but this is an impossible situation."

Julian removed his long-coat, and took some time folding the garment. In exasperation, he tossed it on the trunk. "I agree. I'm not sure what to do."

"We shall remain man and wife, yes?"

"Of that, I have made my decision. For better or worse."

He began unbuttoning his vest. Madeleine blushed, studying him where he stood, not speaking a word. "Madame, what do you look at?"

Her face flamed red; she turned away. "My husband."

He threw his shirt on the trunk, not bothering with the folds. "Only flesh, mine wife." He grinned. "Nothing to cause you embarrassment."

"I've seen such flesh," she said, expressing her worry, turning away, "before…"

"Yes, well, I'm not the type of man to take liberties with an unwilling woman. I'm only preparing for bed."

"I suppose, I should too."

"May I assist you?"

"Do you want to?"

Julian approached her where she stood, and carefully turned her away. Studying her, he breathed her scent, his fingers lingering against the flaxen fabric, sensing the warmth and softness beneath. She would look amazing in silks and satins, a pity she only had this one mulberry gown.

"Julian?"

"Yes?"

"What are you doing?"

"I forgot myself," he said, grasping her stays and releasing them. Whether she was expecting or not, his heart skipped a beat seeing the linen shift beneath. "There you are, your gown is ready to be removed."

She turned to him, holding the sagging fabric to her bosom. "Thank you."

"For what?"

"For being kind." She stepped from her gown, permitting the fabric to fall to the floor. He was still, unsure, she moved closer to him.

She took his hand and squeezed, leaned closer and kissed his cheek. He told himself that the grasp meant little, the kiss less, but he lied, enjoying the quick peck of her lips on his cheek.

"I don't want to take further advantage or beg for some sort of kindness you're not prepared to give. I only mean to thank you for caring for me, and my child. You could have abandoned us, but you chose to keep us safe."

He nodded.

"Julian, if you wish to partake of womanly pleasures, I will give myself to you."

He reflected on the invitation, his mouth watering, his penis hardening, twitching. He did find her attractive, but he wasn't ready for more. Not yet.

"No." He turned away, if only to hide the truth, his body's betrayal.

He heard her sigh of resignation. "I expected rejection, but I'm surprised at how much it hurts."

"I cannot. One look at your belly and…"

"Of course, copulating with an expectant woman is not…"

"Madeleine, nothing has changed."

Madeleine stood before her husband in her shift, coping with the rejection dimming his eyes. Sighing, she walked to the bed and climbed beneath the coverlets. Julian removed his breeches and did the same, climbing beneath the sheets as well.

Quiet, not speaking, they lay beside each other, staring at the wood-slatted ceiling. Suddenly, Madeleine turned onto her side, away from Julian.

"Good night," she whispered.

"Sleep well," Julian said with a grimace, wanting to touch his wife but hateful pride deterred him from the action. "We have a long journey, come morning."

Madeleine didn't reply.

CHAPTER 20

Madeleine was leaving for the second time in her life. In no hurry to travel the waterways again, she strode along a planked platform, walking toward the wharf, accompanied by her friends, Marie and Geneviève.

The wind breathed warm against her face and the sun shone bright, blinding her. She raised her hand to her brow, shielding her eyesight from the sun and sweeping strands of hair from her eyes, but given her bout of sadness, gray skies could have yielded a precipitous burden of rain and she would not have cared one bit.

She carried the same carpetbag brought with her from France. Everything she owned was inside and the few belongings didn't amount to much. She had yet to use the cutlery, as Julian had hired a cook. She had not confessed that cookery was not one of her best skills, and her embroidering ability was lackluster at best.

When they arrived at the shoreline, her husband was

waiting. She stopped to study him standing near his crew, shouting his orders.

"Stow the gear in the center," Julian called out. "The load is most stable in the middle."

Standing nearby, Madeleine scrutinized the object of his attention. "What type of craft is this?" she asked, considering the vessel lying on the bank, not yet in the water. It was unlike any boat she had ever seen. Long and narrow with a hull that could have been stripped from a tree, she wondered where she would sit. Wondered why they were not taking a longboat.

"Birch-bark," he said, gesturing to it with his hand. "A canoe." As if the information satisfied her, he returned to his work, keeping his back to her, his hands on his hips. The sentiment made her feel small and insignificant.

"Every man is to keep his musket at the ready, the powder horn full, his sword housed in its sheath at his side."

Madeleine glanced briefly at the weapon slung low on her husband's hips, hoping he would have no need to use it. Geneviève dashed off to her husband while Marie, suddenly at her side, pressed close.

"It's a canoe—chérie," she giggled, poking Madeleine in the side. "Brighten up. Someone must have risen from the wrong side of the bed. I suppose this means the good captain has not happily engaged his wife and trouble is still afoot."

"He's otherwise occupied, and our conversations only lead to further avoidance. Our interactions don't offer much more than curt dismissals, and his temperament has not changed if that's what you're referring to."

Julian must have heard the comment for he turned to her,

his face marred with irritation. But perhaps he was a man of patience, for though not amused, he returned to his work and the preparations taking place.

Undeterred, Marie pressed closer. "You must give him a sample of your wares; only a taste, mind you. Look at him," she whispered, gesturing with her gloved fingers, "he's but a man starved of affection. Anyone can see it. Burly like a bear! Hungry for a piece of fish."

"More like a fatted pie," Madeleine responded, shaking her head. "He will be disappointed when he learns I cannot cook. But never mind me, what of you? Tell me of your new husband. Are you happy?"

"He's given me a reason to smile." Marie smirked, pondering the man in question.

"At least he acknowledges your exchange when you smile at him."

"He smiles at every pretty skirt that way, and there's few women to turn a man's head in this new country. I'm concerned actually, though, perhaps I imagine issues without merit."

"A woman knows these things; we have our sensibilities."

"I hope I'm not worrying overly, but I fear my husband's a ladies' man, even if he does enjoy my company."

Madeleine shook her head. "A sad situation we're in. One man who's hungry for his wife's attention and the other, hungry for the next adventure. I suppose men will be men regardless of the port of call."

"It appears so."

"LET ME HELP YOU," Julian said, taking Madeleine's bag and stowing it inside the canoe. He was so close to her, Madeleine contemplated his staid expression, wanting more than he could give, and wishing she could say something that might make a difference.

"You don't have to assist me. I can manage. Just tell me where to place my foot in this hold."

"My crew would not understand a slight against my wife. Come, take my hand. I won't let you fall. Step, right there, and sit in front of this cross bar."

"Kind of you to assist me," Madeleine said, grasping his hand. She studied his hazel eyes, wavering on feeble legs, but he did not let her fall. His grip on her fingers was strong; his free hand supported the small of her back, causing tiny shivers to tickle her spine, but he easily assisted her over the gunwale and inside the canoe.

"Madeleine, I will have your care, whether I want the responsibility or not. I mind my officers' welfare, anything less for my wife would be seen as disrespectful."

"Despite everything, I appreciate your kindness. I wish..."

Sighing, he stepped away, obviously considering what she had said. "I see what you want, for now, I will ensure you're well cared for," he said, gazing in the direction they would travel. "I will watch over you."

"Should I be concerned? Of the journey, of what we might face?"

"We will exercise caution. I don't want you to worry, but there are rough waters ahead. Best you sit, you're about to leave port."

"Men—" Julian called out, grabbing the canoe's stern, "move the canoes into the water."

The officers complied with his command and soon all three boats were in the river. The canoe wobbled on the water as Julian climbed inside. He sat behind her on the stern seat, his legs tucked under the support. The voyage was awkward at first. Madeleine tried to sit tall and straight of back, not wanting to encounter her husband's thighs, so she focused on the assembled group of people instead.

Three birch-bark canoes carried a group of eighteen men and three women on the journey upstream along la Rivière Saint-Laurent. In the captain's vessel, four officers sat mid-length, one officer in the bow seat, and Julian and herself took up the rear. Marie and Geneviève's canoes were managed in the same way.

"Stroke," Julian ordered, setting the paddle's rhythm while assisting with the steering. Madeleine watched the officers dip their oars into the water, pulling, propelling the canoe forward. They sailed swiftly along la Rivière Saint-Laurent, the men making the work appear easy.

Large men with strong muscular arms continuously drove their paddles in the water, pulling them upstream. Boredom soon muddled her mind. She stared at the water, then across the distance to study a thick copse of shrubbery and elm trees lining the shore. They were thick with greenery and she could scarcely see between their trunks, or for that matter, what lay beyond. Someone could easily hide beneath the branches, crouching, waiting. The vision frightened her.

Her back soon hurt; her shoulders ached. She shrugged, trying not to alert Julian to her discomfort.

"Lean backward," he said, placing the paddle on his knees, grasping her shoulder, squeezing the aching muscles. "Let me take your weight." Grateful, she glanced at him.

"Come now, trust me. Let me ease your discomfort."

"I'm heavy," she said, biting at her lip, twisting to see him better.

"Quite heavy," he mused, breaking into a grin, the first smile she had seen in days. "However heavy with child, you're still a willow bending in the wind."

"A willow?"

"A tree, a shrub. The point I'm trying to make is that you're reed thin. You could use some fattening up, for the sake of the, well, the child. He or she will need a healthy mother."

She turned away, stretching backward, accepting the sensation of his upper legs. "Julian, perhaps you should not speak so loud. Someone might hear."

"Does it matter? There's no reason to be ashamed."

"That's not true, Julian. I know how people judge, how people talk. I was once a lady after all, a woman born into a life of privilege."

"No offense meant. Sweet heaven, you're showing, mine wife. I will not have secrets between us. Nor will I hide the truth from my officers, especially when the truth is starting to show."

She looked at him, her face flaming pink. "Do they know?"

"Most have guessed. I have been an honest man my entire life. I will not shelter you with lies."

"Oh," Madeleine whispered, lowering her head.

"People were bound to learn the truth. I was going to find out. I have accepted my lot. You must too."

"Have I not?"

He leaned toward her and grasped her chin, surprising her when he raised her sights, forcing her to take in his indulgent expression. "You do not meet your fate by studying your feet. Gaze beyond the mark, consider your future."

"You're a kind man, Julian."

"Do not hand me the glory just yet," he said in response, releasing his hold to resume his work with the paddle. "We have many leagues to go."

She knew he referred to their relationship. She thought to change the subject. "How far will we travel today?"

"Six, seven hours at most."

"When will we take a break?"

"We've barely had time to build up a good sweat." He grinned, wiping his brow. "Hours to go. We'll break our fast in two, maybe three hours. I have packed pemmican if you become hungry."

"My feet, and my... will be done by then."

"Eventually, we'll reach our destination. Until then, if you need to move around, do so carefully. Canoes can tip and the water is cold."

AFTER A LONG DAY on the river, a group of officers and three women either sat or stood by a bonfire. Madeleine's bottom smarted from several hours spent on the water, so she knelt before the flames, her hands above the heat. Marie sat near her, watching the flames flickering, their appetites having been satisfied by a meal of salted pork and beans.

When someone opened a keg of wine, the conversation became more spirited. Feeling awkward in the presence of men, Madeleine quieted, listening to the officers' jesting about past exploits. One officer had fancied the attention of an aboriginal maiden, another theatrically waved his hands, relating his encounters with the native people; trading goods for beaver pelts on the side or arm to arm combat when a brave warrior had rushed him from the forest.

Madeleine rolled her eyes, not believing the silly tales. To her, the men embellished their stories. A silly game played to get a rise out of three women.

They rattled on—telling accounts of capturing innocent creatures, such as beaver, or worse, womanly pursuits sometimes bordering on rudeness. She shook her head in disgust, and not wanting to cause a stir, wisely remained silent.

When Madeleine could take the rowdy atmosphere no more, she was surprised when an officer brought forth a guitar and another creative soul a flute. The next thing Madeleine knew someone was banging on a drum and everyone was singing. She didn't want to join in, but Marie nudged her in the ribs.

"Come on, Maddie. Live a little." She gave in and added her vocals to the chorus:

Pull on the oars and we glide along together…

She soon found herself enjoying the song. Smiling, she

clapped her hands and tapped her foot against the ground in time to the rhythm.

On my way back from lovely La Rochelle,
I met three maidens,
and all of them were pretty…

Gauvain strode forward and reached for the hand of his new wife. Marie blushed, enjoying the attention, but Madeleine thought the situation comical. His movements were jerky. He cocked forward like a rooster, bouncing as he advanced in some semblance of dancing and with a huge smile lighting his face. He had drunk a few slugs of wine. Madeleine had not consumed any of the liquid herself, guessing noxious fluid hid inside the jug.

But as comical as it seemed, Madeleine soured with jealousy. Marie's face beamed with joy when she accepted Gauvain's grasp. They were soon dancing by the glow of a crimson fire, moonlight above their heads, and other officers clapping their hands.

Geneviève's husband did the same, but the young beauty with eyes the color of amethyst jewels was not much of a dancer either. She moved awkwardly, stepping side to side, though her smile was as great as her eyes, and it seemed like she was enjoying herself.

Madeleine sighed, searching for her husband. She wished he could let his guard down. She saw him sitting opposite her on the other side of the bonfire. He must have been staring at her, for he caught her glance and didn't break the connection. Uncomfortable, she glanced away first.

Fascination must have wet his hunger for he was soon rising, two-stepping, waltzing forward and coming closer to her. His fingers soon urged her chin upward. She gazed at him, lost in the depths of his hazel eyes, astonished he stood before her, wearing an avid expression. The men stopped singing, but their instruments kept up the song, fingers strumming on the strings, flute singing to the moon, compelling further momentum.

"Come on, Julian. Take your bride's hand and give her a whirl," the cook cajoled, "sing to her..."

Madeleine watched her husband with some astonishment, waiting to see what he would do. He opened his mouth and...

I met some pretty maidens,
but I didn't choose any,
I took the prettiest.
I had her mount my saddle,
I went 100 leagues without talking to her.
She asked me for a drink,
and I led her near a fountain...

Madeleine had no words. No man had ever sung to her before.

"Come, dance with me," Julian said with a smile, his attention rapt and fixated on her. She had seen him pour a healthy dose of wine inside his cup. Perhaps the drink drew him to silly lengths. Maybe that's why he posed the question?

"Oh, I could not," she responded, glancing away.

"Come now, don't be shy. You braved a voyage across a

rough sea to find a husband." He beckoned, urging her to rise. "You found me, come to me."

"'Tis true," she said, accepting his outstretched hand. When he pulled her closer to his chest, she went without restraint, closer than was wise.

The music played on, but the two couples stopped dancing. Marie and Gauvain held each other close, one in front of the other, swaying. Geneviève and her beau did the same. Madeleine knew she held everyone's attention, but she wasn't uncomfortable. She only had eyes for her husband, although, she had garnered such attention before. She had sung at the pianoforte for her parents and their guests. Not knowing the true lyrics of this song, Madeleine made up her own, swaying in time to the music, holding her husband's hand and staring into his eyes, she sang:

The water was fresh, so I took a drink.
Gazing at an officer's eyes,
I didn't know what to think.
He caught hold of my hand,
and brought it to his lips…
What else could I do, but let him have his kiss?

Madeleine smiled, a simpering smile as she broke their contact and stepped away, thinking she would sit.

"Ah, none of that, ma chérie." Julian smirked, pulling her back into his embrace. "I don't recall bringing your fingers to my lips, nor do I take kindly to teasing. Will you dance with me?"

He pulled her closer; she soon nestled against his chest,

his strong hand at the small of her back, his fingers urging her closer, his scrutiny causing her heart to flutter. Step touch step, she caught the scent of liquor on his breath, and reflected on the bump lodged between them like a wedge, but they kept up the pretense of the dance.

"I have taken the challenge, Captain, and I feel it's advantageous to step away."

"I will pull you to my side," he said, singing, squeezing her fingers.

"Not if I'm not ready..."

"But, ma chérie, you're my wife."

"You could have chosen from numerous maidens," she said, placing her free hand against his chest.

"I chose the prettiest girl to stand beside me."

"You took me to your castle, and..."

Madeleine admired her husband. A change occurred. Everyone saw the moment when a wife glimpsed tenderness in her husband's eyes. The emotion passed between them, the dancers stopped swaying, the guitarist stopped strumming. Only the flute played the song, but the melody trilled andante, lulling them to a place unseen.

"Julian?"

"Don't spoil the moment," he whispered, standing still.

"I don't understand, what's happening?"

"You don't know?" Julian said with a sigh, his expression earnest. "Your husband has come for you."

"What?" Madeleine hadn't expected his regard. Right in front of his men, he grasped her head with both hands, his fingers sliding in her hair. The embrace warmed her temples and caught her wondering. *Was this a dream? A fantasy? Was this man her husband?* He pressed his advantage further, stepping nearer and kissing her forehead.

"What did I do to deserve your attention?" she asked, closing her eyes, thinking the kiss extraordinary. Soft. Sweet.

"You married me. You chose me. You came to me."

He stepped away, releasing her, leaving her uncertain. Cold without him standing near. "The evening has been entertaining," Julian said to his crew. "But it's time to put the instruments away and call it a night. We rise early in the morning."

"Aye," someone said. "Time to put the pretty maidens to bed."

"Aye," Julian smiled, taking hold of her hand and leading her away from the fire. "I intend on doing just that."

"Where will we sleep?" Madeleine asked, feeling a cool breeze caress her face now that they were separated from the fire's heat.

"Underneath the moon," he grinned, leading her to the canoe, "and beneath the stars."

CHAPTER 21

*J*ulian unfolded the tarpaulin and spread the oilcloth on the ground. Grateful for the moonlight, he knew Madeleine watched him preparing their bed on the forest floor. He glanced at her. Shivering, she clutched at her arms. Night came fast in this country. The daylight hours were lessening and each sunset brought them closer to fall.

Obviously cold, Madeleine didn't complain.

"I have never slept on the ground before."

"You'll either love it or hate it," he said, hoping the latter would not be true. "The nights are cold this time of year. Fall is approaching. I would not travel in the winter when the water's frozen over. A man can lose his toes."

He reached for a thick woolen blanket and stretched it over the tarpaulin. "Will we be cold?" Madeleine asked, stepping nearer to him.

He pondered her whimsical expression, likely still aware of his kiss. "Our body temperatures will help lessen the impact. I take some comfort in the fact I will not be sleeping alone. Come now, lie down. Rest your head at this top point."

Julian took her hand and assisted her to the spread. She was timid, much too quiet. "I see your concern," he said with a grin, "I'll protect you should any wild animals howl at the moon."

As if in response to his taunt, a loon wailed, crooning, somewhere on the river. "If you were thinking to make me less afraid, it's not working."

"My sword arm will be at the ready should wild animals come prowling, but it's hardly the wolves we need be afraid of. You're hearing the song of a loon."

"I'm partial to music, and to your singing, which is strong and good, but if I should have no fear of wolves, what should I fear? Perhaps the native people of this land might cause us concern?"

"Perhaps. I won't lie to you, we're approaching Iroquois hunting grounds. An attack could happen. Not everyone in this new frontier is our friend. Some see us a threat, and with good reason."

He watched her shiver again. "Even with the tarpaulin and the blanket, the ground is cold, and hard."

"Don't worry," Julian said, grasping her foot and gently removing her kid leather slippers. "I'll take your mind off your worries."

Julian removed his boots and stretched out beside Madeleine. He took the blanket edge and wrapped it over and around their feet. It was dark. With only the light of a bulbous moon he covered them until they were cocooned in the coverings.

Now he could feel Madeleine trembling. "I'm cold," she said, shivering, her teeth chattering.

"Come close to me," he urged her, "lean your head on my shoulder. Our body heat will keep us warm."

Madeleine did as he asked and he enjoyed holding her, feeling the weight of her head against his shoulder. "Look at the night sky," he said, his tone optimistic and excited, "take your mind off your worries. Have you ever seen so many stars? An entire clutch of diamonds would not shine as bright."

"They're, they're... amazing," Madeleine stuttered, shifting closer. "A beautiful display."

Julian hugged her to his side, liking the physical nearness. "When I was a boy, I would search the night sky and wonder, wonder what lay beyond, if anything."

"'Tis wondrous to ponder."

Julian pulled his free arm from the coverings. "That star right there, the one to the right," he pointed, gesturing. "More a planet than a star. I wish I could see it. Travel there, like the first explorers to this land."

"Quite impossible, I think."

"In our generation, perhaps. Someday, a ship might sail to the moon."

Her teeth stopped chattering. "Do you ever search the heavens, Madeleine, and if so, what do you see and what do you hope for?"

"As a child, I was more fascinated by the light of day. I would lie on my back and gaze at blue skies cluttered with clouds. I watched them change shape, curling and unfurling..."

"And…"

"My life was simpler then. A time when a pretty gown enhanced my figure, making me feel like a lady."

"You're still a lady. I hear it in every word you speak. Your intonation provides evidence of your social class. A time in your life when the days were better, and a woman could dream."

"I was happy once. Sometimes life is cruel and rewards you with scratchy linen instead of fine muslin."

Julian pulled her closer, beneath his chin, closer to his heart. "You cannot measure the worth of a person by the clothes they wear, but if I'm ever a rich man, I will buy you a gown fit for a ladies figure. I will see you happy again."

"'Tis funny, I was a glutton for finer things, expensive dresses, pretty jewels. They are trinkets to me now. They do not matter anymore."

"That's good," Julian mused, "because I'm not a rich man. If I were, I would not be in this new land in the first place."

"Why did you come to New France, Julian?"

"To serve my country and escape the curse of being born a second son. Though if I'm to confess the truth, I had a will to explore. I could not travel to the stars or to the moon, so I came to this country instead. Purely selfish reasons."

"And the woman you profess to love, the one you left behind in France?"

"She would have hated it here. I see that now."

"But you loved her."

"She's a part of my past and best left there. Are you warming up?"

"Yes."

"Good. It's time to sleep. Rest. We have another long journey tomorrow."

He pulled the tarpaulin over their heads, but left enough space that they would not breathe into the coverings. "Good night, Madeleine."

"Night," Madeleine yawned, soon quiet, not talking.

She was soon fast asleep. Julian listened to her breathing, the sweet hush of in and out and the calming sounds of water trickling nearby. She nestled closer and he became aware of her warm breath against his neck. He craned his head nearer to her, welcoming the sensation, breathing the sweet perfume of violets lingering in her hair. He closed his eyes, recognizing he had been alone for too long. He never wanted to be alone again.

He could father her child—

"Sweet dreams," he whispered. Fast asleep, Madeleine could not hear him.

"I would like to be a voyageur, too," Madeleine mumbled, pressing closer still. "The stars, you see…"

"I will take you there," he said with a grin, closing his eyes. "To the moon and back, someday."

CHAPTER 22

*M*adeleine opened her eyes, awakening to the sunlight dappling against the river with the twitter of birdsong filling the air. Several days had passed. The group of voyageurs had settled into a familiar routine, and this day was no different from the last. With the sunrise, the camp sprang into action. In no hurry to rise, Madeleine watched Julian and the other officers climbing from their bedrolls and efficiently disassembling them.

Their work should have consumed her with guilt, but comfortable inside her tarpaulin and thick woolen blanket, she didn't want to leave the warmth of her wrapping yet.

"Come now—" Julian scolded, smiling. "It's time to break camp. Wipe the sleep from your eyes. Pull yourself from your safe harbor."

"Oh, come on, Julian," she groaned, stretching her arms high above her head. "The sun has barely risen; the ground will be cold against my feet."

"My hands are full, or I would find my pleasure pulling you from your cocoon."

She rolled to her side to scrutinize her husband. "You have something for me?"

"Put your shoes on and place your wrapper around your shoulders. I have a hot drink to warm you from the inside."

"Kind of you to think of me, but I'm comfortable here and I don't see any reason why a few more moments of shut-eye should matter."

"Now, now, pretty maiden," he said with a grin, sidling closer, "you must obey your captain. Everyone in the camp heeds my orders when it's time to break camp. What would my subordinates think if my own wife didn't agree to do my bidding?"

"Unlike your officers," Madeleine giggled, adoring his winsome smile, "I'm not permitted to perform any chores. You forbade it. I'm not complaining, mind you, but this one morning permit me to enjoy this glorious view for a few moments more. My bottom still holds the impressions of yesterday's journey."

"We will have a break soon. Fort Richelieu is in sight. We'll sleep in our own bedchamber, and share a real bed, tonight."

Madeleine would have replied but his earnest expression gave her pause. She had slept beside her husband for days and he was a complete gentleman every night. But she could see his attitude had changed. He looked at her differently. Stared at her when she wasn't aware of his notice. She knew his look of desire and what his attention meant.

"Oh, very well." Madeleine gave in, taking Julian's hand

and permitting him to assist her to her feet. She shivered when the wind blew cold against her cheeks. She slipped her kid leather shoes on her feet, soon wrapping the woolen blanket around her shoulders.

"Take this," Julian remarked, placing a cup of hot tea in her hand.

She accepted the pewter cup, then walked to a fallen log and sat on the bark, sipping the beverage. "It's strong as always, but I'll not complain."

The cook brought her a plate of cooked peas and salted pork. The meal had been cooking all night, the scent carrying on the wind, encouraging her hunger. She accepted a spoon and began to eat, while contemplating Julian folding their thick woolen blanket, followed by the tarpaulin. It was wrong to watch him toiling while she satisfied her hunger, but he didn't seem to mind. She placed the cup and plate on the ground and went to him.

"Please let me help, Julian."

He glanced at her momentarily, and then continued his work. "Finish your meal, save your strength for later. Your condition is delicate. I can handle this."

"I'm with child, I'm not useless. But regardless of my condition, I'm capable of helping you."

"I don't want to return to our past worries."

"I appreciate your concern, for myself and for my unborn child, but I have had no further cramping or bleeding. I could help with the meals? Yes? Marie and Geneviève assist with the gathering of kindling, assembling the camp, sometimes minding the fire while I watch, leaving me feeling useless. I should help."

"The cook is able to perform his duties without your help, but if you insist," he said, stepping toward her with the tarpaulin tucked underneath his arm, "you could possibly do something more pleasurable and become a proper wife when we arrive at Fort Richelieu."

"Oh," she said, her cheeks heating. "And what does it mean to become a proper wife?"

"What do you want it to mean?" he asked, smirking, glancing away then meeting her expression again.

"I'm not sure if we're talking about cooking a meal, tending a home, or something more, more sensitive? I have not contemplated wanton needs since, well, we were married."

"Finish your breakfast. We can consider what it means to coexist when we don't share our bedchamber with everyone else."

Madeleine ventured to the log and retrieved her plate, spooning peas and salted pork in her mouth. "At night, the many people in our encampment have not hindered Marie and Gauvain's attentiveness."

"You heard them, too?"

"Julian, I cannot believe we're having this conversation. It's unnatural."

"Conversations between a husband and his wife are important. Every day we strengthen our relationship, and seem to like each other a bit more. I'm enjoying getting to know the real you," he laughed, coming to stand at her feet. "Madeleine, you're red in the face, you're fetching when your cheeks are red with emotion. It makes me want to touch your cheeks."

"Julian, you're my husband, but you've pressed your point far enough."

"I'd like to press forward with a much different advance."

"Oh, you would? What type of advance?"

"Well," he said, raking his fingers through his hair. "You've pressed your sweet little bottom against my groin for several nights in a row, and *ma chérie*, forgive me for saying so, but my needs have grown with each contact. You're not only beautiful, you're also my sweet little wife, and I want you."

She stopped eating. "You want to assert your marital rights?"

"If you think the child would not suffer."

"You're asking this of me?"

He came closer; he knelt before her on the ground, taking her cup, holding her hand. "It's not the birdsong whistling in your ear, it's your husband kneeling beneath your curious perusal."

"We're in the company of your officers and my friends. Should we discuss such matters while they can overhear our conversation?"

"Later tonight, if you're willing, maybe we can see what could happen?" He winked, rising. "See where the pleasure takes us when we have our privacy."

Madeleine didn't know what to say so she wisely remained silent. Their relationship was growing closer each day and she was glad of it. But this new friendship with her husband filled her with fear, fear that she would be a disappointment. They had come so far, grown closer. She sucked in a breath, hoping she could find the courage to fulfill her husband's needs. After all, it was his right.

JULIAN GAVE Madeleine much to consider. After breaking their fast, the officers broke camp, loaded the gear inside the canoes and then set them on the river. Madeleine took her spot inside, grimacing, sitting on the woolen blanket, focusing on what lay ahead.

The voyage upriver would soon end, but she wasn't relieved of her concerns, as her husband would welcome a new intimacy in their relationship.

"Let me assist you inside the canoe."

She grasped Julian's hand, glimpsing his passion as he helped her over the canoe's lip, assisting her to sit. They were soon adrift on the river, traveling upstream.

"Are you comfortable?" he asked, paddling in time with the other officers.

"Yes," she lied, shifting position. He licked his lips, noticing her discomfort.

"Stroke," Julian called out. "Let's get these girls to the fort. A change in scenery will do everyone good."

CHAPTER 23

Inside the commanding officer's quarters at Fort Richelieu, Julian stood next to a gray stone hearth, holding his slouch hat in his hands. He understood the importance of the mission and his travel mandate to Fort Sainte-Anne, but he had a wife to consider now. Conflict or not, he had to keep Madeleine safe.

"I'm aware the Mohawk warriors have attacked the outpost. René told me about the conflict before I left Ville de Québec."

"Then what's to discuss?" Henri said, sitting at a pine table a short distance away. "I recognize the crown coerced you into marriage, but you didn't come to New France to protect a wife. You and your men may have a night's rest and then you must continue with your mission. As planned."

"I didn't ask for this marriage but now that I have a wife," Julian said, turning away from the hearth, "I must see to her welfare. She's with child. The journey's been difficult on her."

"Your wife doesn't concern me, what does is replenishing

the officers at Fort Sainte-Anne. Seven of our men were slain, four were taken."

"I must think of my wife."

"Captain Benoit, please take a seat at the table. I feel like I'm talking to a mountain."

Julian did as requested. He placed his hat on his knee and waited for Henri to speak again.

"Look, I must address the greater cause. You're using your wife as a shield, as an excuse to shirk your duties. It's poor form. Regardless of your marital commitments, you have a duty to the regiment. I will not discharge you from your responsibilities."

"I have never shirked my duties; I understand my charge and I'm prepared to fulfill my obligations."

"Then why are we having this conversation? Do you want to leave your wife at Fort Richelieu while you complete your duties? You have days yet to travel and you could be stationed at Fort Sainte-Anne for months. Isn't it better to have your wife with you?"

"A month ago, I didn't have a wife, didn't have this concern wrapped around my neck."

"Ah, so you move fast, my friend," Henri chuckled, slapping the table with his hand.

"Faster than you know," Julian blurted, choosing to keep the truth to himself.

"Look, officers who have wifely responsibilities cannot be assigned non-military duties. Granting reprieves from an officer's workload was never the intent in bringing women to New France, but you're not alone in your grievances. Many soldiers have taken on the burden at the urging of Jean Talon and the king, for the colony's sake. It's an ill-advised business. First, we bring our officers to New France to assist with the conflicts of the native people, and then we saddle them with responsibility."

"I didn't mind overly," Julian admitted, drumming his fingers on the table. "We're finally starting to understand each other."

"It's made you and your fellow officers happier having your beds warmer at night, having a companion to share your burdens with, but it's also complicated regimental matters," Henri said with a frown, rising from his chair. "Would you like a cognac? I find these conversations easier to swallow with a strong drink."

"I wouldn't mind, actually."

"Let me help you with your decisions. So, here's our issue. The Mohawk people, allies with the British colonials, refuse to take the peace offerings. These Iroquois aggressors are not alone with their concerns. The Oneida are also hesitant to attend the peace talks. We must force them to see reason."

"How do you plan on doing that?"

Henri reached into a wooden cabinet and grabbed a snifter. He poured a healthy dose of cognac into two cut-glass beakers. "Intendant Jean Talon has weighed the pros and cons of the mission and has concluded that we must go on the offensive. Courcelle and Tracy are in complete agreement with his assessment."

"It's the end of summer. Pardon me for saying this, Commander, but the last campaign was futile. How many officers did we lose?"

"True enough, but we won't deliberate foolish maneuvers.

Everyone believed it was a joke, a disastrous idea with the advent of winter, but Courcelle wouldn't see reason. It's safe to say, we won't make the same mistake again."

"What's the course of action?"

Henri passed a crystal glass into Julian's hand. "Plans are being made to challenge the Mohawk," he said, sitting, swallowing a good amount of cognac. "This is the reason we're sending you to Fort Sainte-Anne. We want you to assist with the war mission. Lead a patrol into Mohawk lands."

"Patrols into Mohawk land, into their territory?" Julian took a swallow of cognac, worrying what his officers might face. He didn't like this situation at all.

"You bet. An expedition advancing into their territory, seeking their villages and their warriors. If the Iroquois won't see reason, if they continue to harm our officers, our colonists, then we have no other choice. They threaten our livelihood, our people. This is war, I'm afraid. We must stand up for the cause."

Julian took a deep breath, seeing the serious expression on the commander's face. This was a serious business they were confronting. "My wife will be in danger at Fort Sainte-Anne."

"Your wife will be safe enough within the fort's walls, but no wandering beyond the gates or by the river where our officers were attacked. No place is safe while the Iroquois wreak their havoc, attacking us when least expected. Savage warfare tactics, and they're damn good at it."

Julian sighed, seeing he had no other choice but to take Madeleine with him.

"If it helps, I'll give you one more day here, but no more than that. Do not leave your wife helpless. Teach her how to load and fire a musket. Give her lessons with a sword while you're at it. She might need to defend herself."

"I suppose I have no other choice."

"Don't look so petulant. You're an officer," Henri said, swirling the amber liquid in his glass, soon taking another gulp. "You've been trained to handle these operations, but I have concerns with you traveling south, too. Mack is here. He will be your guide as promised, help you make your way to Fort Sainte-Anne."

"I appreciate his assistance. Calms my concerns somewhat."

"Tell me something, Captain Benoit. Do you love this woman?"

"Love? That's a strong word, but I do care for her, Commander."

"Then take care of her."

"I'll do my best, Sir." Julian rose from the table, took a hard swallow of cognac, then placed the glass on the table.

"I wish you well, Captain, and I thank you for your service."

"You're welcome," Julian replied, preparing to leave, placing his hat on his head.

"Take advantage of the quarters I've assigned you. A young man should go into battle having known his pleasure."

Julian's face turned red. "Thank you for your gift, Henri. Madeleine will be grateful for a real bed."

"It's you who should be grateful. Sleep well, Julian."

He left the commander's quarters set on sleeping beside his wife, but would he do more than find his rest? He was ready for intimacy, but was Madeleine?

CHAPTER 24

*M*adeleine was grateful for the privacy, warmth, and comfort of the officer's quarters. Alone in the small chamber, she reclined on a linen mattress filled with wool, watching a tallow candle. The flame flickered on the wick, dancing against the whitewashed walls. Having nothing else to pass the time, she watched the illumination, wondering when Julian would join her in their chamber and what might happen when he came to share this bed.

He expected intimacy, though sharing anything more than a hug or a kiss made her uncomfortable, nervous. As if in response to her concerns, the door opened, and Julian entered the chamber.

"You're still awake," he said, soon closing the door. He seemed upset, perhaps he had worries of his own.

"I was waiting for you," she said, taking a deep breath, hoping to disguise her anxiety. "You're troubled, is it because of me?"

"No, of course not." He removed his slouch hat and brown long-coat and laid both on a chair, then came nearer to her and sat at the foot of the bed. "I had a meeting with the fort's commander. I'm sorry to say, I bring troubling news."

"Whatever it is, you can tell me."

He studied her seriously, a grave expression stealing the color from his eyes. He grasped her ankle. "I have not been completely honest with you regarding our journey to Fort Sainte-Anne. I have misled you by concealing the truth of my mission."

"You would never intentionally mislead without good reason. Whatever it is, you'll tell me when the time is right. Though it's only fair my husband is honest with me, too."

"I appreciate your courtesy and your trust."

"Julian," Madeleine soothed, seeing his worry, "if you're concerned about sharing your news, I can face whatever you need to say. We're in danger, are we not? Is it the native people? Will they attack us when we journey further south?"

"You're perceptive. We will be in danger when we travel to Fort Sainte-Anne. The Iroquois, the Mohawk people, attacked a group of officers fishing near the fort a few weeks ago. They murdered some of our officers and abducted four others. I should not be telling you this, but we travel to the fort to assist the officers who remain, and to support the war mission."

"Oh," Madeleine said, wondering what she would do if forced to face such terrors. "How do you feel about this mission? Does it worry you?"

Julian released her ankle and rose from the bed.

Madeleine watched him remove his white lawn shirt. "Not for myself. I need to take my wife into account. Your safety is my primary concern."

"It's considerate of you to care for my well-being."

"I have promised to protect you. I don't want anyone to cause you harm. We will not travel tomorrow. I have received permission to stay at the fort for at least one more day."

"I'm grateful. It's a welcome reprieve to sleep in a real bed."

"I'm looking forward to the comfort myself, despite the fact I like to rest beneath the stars."

He turned, staring, then came to lie beside her. She made a space for him. "Come here, ma chérie, lay your head on my shoulder."

Madeleine did as she was asked, but the possibility of intimacy worried her, so she lay stiffly against him.

"Come now," he said, somehow recognizing her discomfort, "relax. It's time we explored being a real couple, but I will not rush you. Our relationship will proceed as it's meant to."

"It still feels strange being married."

"Do you favor me, Madeleine? Or are we working toward an intimacy that can never be?"

"I care for you, Julian. We are finally becoming friends, you and me. But the baby…"

"What about the baby? Our relationship has nothing to do with the child."

"Doesn't it?" Madeleine asked, taking a deep breath. "My condition is like a wedge lodged between us."

"It doesn't have to be," Julian said, placing his hand on her burgeoning stomach. The baby moved beneath his touch. "I can accept this child, be a father to this child. I'm starting to have feelings for its mother."

He was serious. Madeleine stared at his handsome hazel eyes. He didn't shy away from her scrutiny. "How could I have been so fortunate to have found a man like you?" Madeleine's voice choked with emotion, tears filled her eyes, she cupped his cheek with her hand. "I could love a man such as you."

He smiled. "I would like to be loved. I've waited a long time to find love. May I kiss you?"

"Yes, you may."

Madeleine was slightly anxious. Only one man had kissed her mouth and his dirty lips had been sloppy, wet with greed, and lusting only for her intimate parts. She tried not to think about the horrible memories, but when Julian stroked her neck, she remembered the abuse. Her father's friend, his stale mouth, his pelvis rutting on top of her, rocking her into his mattress, forcing her legs apart with his knees. It was too much. Breathing heavily, she pulled away.

"What is it?" Julian asked, pausing.

"It's nothing."

"Is it me? Do my actions make you uncomfortable?"

"It's not you, Julian."

"Then what? You must tell me."

Madeleine didn't know what to say. The past had been hidden for so long and now it came between them, no different than her condition, though Julian was a clever man.

She could not dishonor him with lies, she must confess her truth.

"Madeleine, I shan't force you to accept my caresses when you're clearly uncomfortable with my touch. But I would never hurt you, yes?"

"Yes," she said with a whimper, "I think so."

"Come to me. I want *you* to kiss me. I will not touch you while you do it."

"What's wrong with me? You're my husband."

"I understand. Someone forced himself on you. I will not force myself on my wife, but we could share something beautiful, when you're ready. You take the first step. You come to me."

"So, I should kiss you?"

"If you're comfortable. A test of faith?"

Madeleine moved closer to her husband. She placed her hand on Julian's naked chest and gazed into his eyes. *I'm not afraid of this man. He has never done anything to cause me concern.* His heart beat beneath her hand, slow and steady. His skin was warm to the touch. He smiled, perhaps in encouragement.

"Your eyes are heavenly, Julian."

"I know," he said, grinning, "all the ladies tell me."

"They do?"

"No distractions. Do you want to kiss me?"

She strained forward, studying his lips. She did want to kiss him, so she closed her eyes and pressed her lips against his mouth, touching more than kissing. He didn't make any attempt to touch her.

"How did you like it?"

Madeleine sighed. "Butterflies may have flirted with my insides."

"That's the baby," Julian snickered, his breath so close it whispered against her lips. "Do you want to sample my lips again?"

"I would not mind." The second attempt, Madeleine kissed her husband, enjoying the caress. "Nice," she said, leaning her head against his forehead.

Julian pulled her into his embrace, kissing her nose. "You may kiss me as often as you wish, we'll progress at a slower pace to further lovemaking. Nothing more than sweet kisses from my wife's lips tonight."

"I'm sorry to keep you waiting."

"No apologies necessary. You've suffered a trauma. I don't want you thinking about anyone else while we're together. When you're ready, I want you to desire me, to want me to touch you anywhere and everywhere, and be comfortable with the experience."

"How did you know I was remembering, the ah, painful experience with my father's gambling friend?"

"I didn't. I realized there was a barrier. I imagine a woman who has suffered abuse at the hands of another man might be uncomfortable with intimacy. I understand."

"I'm not uncomfortable being with you."

"I know."

"How?" Madeleine asked, perplexed.

"You kissed me, chérie."

"Oh, true enough."

"I will take some time tomorrow to teach you how to defend yourself should the need arise. Not only from the first people of this land, but also because of men who might seek to do you harm. Do you think you could handle a musket? A sword? You're a small woman. I'm not sure if you can hold a musket, they're heavy."

"I'll manage it, because as you've said, there's a threat and I might need to protect myself."

"If the man who abused you ever shows his face in New France, I'll gut him myself."

"Let's not speak of it. Will Marie and Geneviève participate in the lesson?"

"Yes. You should all be prepared, just in case."

Julian moved closer still, she felt his nose against her cheek. "May I hold you while we sleep?"

She smiled despite herself, feeling more comfortable. "You're my husband, 'tis your right."

"Come. Turn onto your side, lie beside me. Let me hold you."

Madeleine rolled to her side, and Julian nestled close. She became aware of every part of his body. His arm draped over her waist, his fingers massaging her protruding belly. He became quiet. His warm breath whispered against her neck, tickling her earlobe.

"May I kiss you good night, ma chérie?"

She turned to him, seeing his serene expression. His thumb pad stroked her cheek, his lips descended on her mouth. He kissed her. A yearning ignited from somewhere inside her heart and she returned his kiss.

He pulled away, placing his head on his pillow.

"That was beautiful."

"Yes, it was."

Madeleine wanted more but chose not to tell Julian. Her emotions were conflicted, wet with need. Soon, she listened to his breathing, the comforting sound of soft inhalations as he breathed. *Peace.* She had somehow found a new hope. This was her last thought as she succumbed to sleep.

CHAPTER 25

*M*adeleine tried to listen to Julian as he taught a lesson on weaponry to the group; but concentrating was difficult. She strained to hear his voice, knowing this lesson was important. There were many reasons why she should be more alert, but she was caught up in her husband's physicality, his attractive face, his muscular build.

Focus, Madeleine, focus!

He held a flintlock musket in his hands, his face lined with the significance, his demeanor conveying a respect for the weapon. He mastered the iron; she considered his physical strength while holding its power. But knowing her intimately? Holding her? She gritted her teeth, wondering how she might permit him to touch a part of her that had been stolen by another.

His left hand held the barrel; the right held the stock. She remembered the previous evening; when Julian's fingers had stroked her shoulder, her face, her lips. A new sensation, a kindness, a tenderness had enveloped her. Madeleine heated, recalling his touch.

"This moment is important. So pay attention. We're about to learn how to load the musket," Julian said with some seriousness, stepping toward Madeleine and passing the musket into her hands.

"I expected the musket would be heavy, but how will I hold this metal beast?"

"I hope you won't have to use it," he said, holding the weapon between them, "but if you're threatened, you will not hesitate to pull the trigger. Understand? I will protect you as best I can, but you must have the strength of mind to hold and fire the weapon."

"Julian. You're frightening me."

"The hardest trigger you'll ever pull is the one that saves your life and ends someone else's. Sometimes, it must be done." He paused, staring at her meaningfully. "Ladies, three points to be aware of in this demonstration; the muzzle, the chamber and the stock of the weapon. The chamber needs powder for the charge to ignite after the hammer strikes the flint and creates a spark. The muzzle requires powder. Don't forget this. Do you understand, ladies?"

"Yes," Madeleine, Geneviève and Marie replied.

"Load the musket, Gauvain."

"Hold the weapon against the ground and between your feet. Retrieve the cartridge," Gauvain said, taking a small packet from his powder horn. "Tear the cartridge, biting the edge with your teeth, then pour the powder inside muzzle. Follow with the paper, placing it on the barrel edge like this," he said, making a nest, "add the ball, reach for your ramrod, then tamp the cartridge all the way down the barrel."

Holding her musket against the ground, Madeleine hoped she would remember the steps.

"Ladies, you've watched Gauvain load his musket. Are you ready to give it a try?"

"It appears easy enough," Madeleine said, loading her musket, tamping the works inside the barrel. "But with the gun's weight, this is no easy task, and I'm moving much too slow."

"It's not terrible," Marie said, tamping her cartridge.

"Have you done this before, Marie? You seem at ease with your weapon."

"I may have had cause to shoot in the past and I will not hesitate to use a weapon in the future, should the need arise."

"Excellent, you have experience." Julian praised her, seemingly surprised. "I didn't expect it. What comes next?"

"Yes. Pull the frizzen back, like this," Marie said, carrying out the action. "Then pour a bit of powder in the pan, close the frizzen, pull back the hammer and set your sights on the enemy, like…" She drew the musket upward, pointing…

"Oh no, chérie," Gauvain said, snickering as if it was a joke, placing his hand on the barrel. "Never point a loaded weapon anywhere near your husband. I was afraid you would fire."

"I could, you know. I could fire the weapon, setting my sights on the perfect target."

"That's great," Julian said, his eyebrows raised. "I don't know where you received your training, but I'm grateful there's one less woman to teach."

"I cannot do this." Geneviève whimpered, dropping her musket on the ground like a child might in frustration. "It's too heavy. I'll never be able to manage it, never mind load it. I'm going to die."

Jacques Meneu, her husband, came to her aid and retrieved the musket from the ground. "Now, now, ma chére, there are other ways to fight these battles. The blade is lighter to carry and better placed."

"You want me to use a knife?"

"Or a sword."

"I cannot stick someone," Geneviève complained. "I would not harm a mouse."

"We will do what we must, should trouble arise," Julian said to the group. "We're not facing small creatures, after all. Madeleine, do you want to fire the gun?"

She nodded.

"Bring up your weapon," Julian ordered, coming behind her. He stood so close she could hear his breathing. "Hold the musket butt against your shoulder, support it with your cheek. Do you know what comes next?"

"Pull the hammer back to half-cock," Madeleine said, hearing the click of metal lock into place.

Julian came nearer, keeping her close while he helped her steady the weapon. The proximity of his well-muscled body pressed against her back caused acute awareness. She could hear his breathing and felt his warm breath blowing against her neck. It took every bit of her willpower to focus on the musket.

"We're aiming for the pot hanging from the tree. Are you ready?"

"Yes."

"Fire on my command."

"Julian, I'm not an officer."

"Today, my darling, you're an officer. Fire!"

Bang! Madeleine flinched as the musket fired. The barrel propelled into her shoulder and she gasped. A distinct ping was heard as the ball met its mark. White smoke filled the air and her eyes filled with tears.

"Excellent shot. You struck gold, Madeleine."

"Only because you helped me. I could not have done it on my own."

"Of course, you could have. Shall we try again?"

"All right."

Madeleine reached for a cartridge from her powder horn, following the steps, soon tamping the load in the barrel. After loading the pan, she closed the frizzen, pulled back the hammer and raised the gun, holding it against her shoulder. Squinting, she sought the mark.

I can do this... she told herself, bearing the weight, massaging the trigger with her finger.

"Fire," Julian yelled.

Bang. Ping! Madeleine smiled, realizing she had hit the mark twice. In her excitement, she turned to face Julian, still holding the musket. He appeared happy, delighted with the outcome. "I did it. On my own."

He took the musket from her hands. "You sure did. I'm proud of you."

Marie stepped forward. "Look at you, Maddie girl, a woman in a new land firing a weapon like a pro."

"A greenhorn more like, I'm slow with the loading and

unaccustomed to holding a weapon. How will I manage in a real scenario? And Marie, my friend with her firing secrets. Where did you learn to load and fire a musket?"

Marie grinned, gazing at her husband. "Someone in my life might have believed that gun handling was necessary. However," she said, stepping close, whispering… "I'll tell you my secret someday, when the timing is right."

"First, you must prove you can fire it, Marie."

Marie stepped a few paces from the mark, raised her weapon and fired. *Bang*. Ping! She looked like a woman born to hold a weapon, achieving the action so smoothly. Her ball met its mark, too.

"Well done," Gauvain said. But Marie disregarded his comment.

"Your turn, Geneviève."

"I'm sorry, I cannot do it."

"Geneviève," her husband said, "this is for your own safety."

Her face crumpled and she began to cry.

"It's all right, my darling. Don't cry. It's enough that two of our ladies can shoot, right Captain?"

"To be fair, I'd be happier if everyone could fire their muskets, but I will not push. A man doesn't like to see a woman cry. What about a knife?" Julian asked, stepping toward Geneviève, "do you think you could slide a blade into a gunny sack?"

"I could try," she said, her lower lip quivering.

He pulled a blade from his side and passed it over, handle first.

"Hit it hard," Julian said.

She approached the sack but could not get the knife through the fabric.

"Oh for heaven's sake," Marie exclaimed, taking the knife from her hands. "Put some strength into your muscle. Get angry, strike, and shove this stick into the sack."

Marie thrust with all her might, sliding the metal into the sack. She left it there, grinning. Madeleine was amazed at her strength but didn't think to question her skill.

"You are a wonder, Marie. And full of surprises."

"Madeleine, I'll not have my hair taken by anyone with a savage nature. I will protect myself. This is a serious business."

"Lesson over for today," Julian said, appearing frustrated. "Do not forget what you've learned today. We leave in the morning."

"To ride in the strange canoe."

"And walk, too. Come Madeleine. We'll sup in our room, privately."

CHAPTER 26

*M*adeleine studied the officers, scrutinizing rippling biceps as they drove their paddles into the churning water, propelling them upstream along la Rivière Richelieu.

"Stroke, stroke, stroke," Julian called out, driving the crew continually forward.

Sitting semi-comfortably in the boat, Madeleine heard a shrill, screeching cry. When the strident tone disturbed her hearing a second time, she twisted in the canoe, soon sighting an eagle soaring with the breeze, drifting among a cerulean-blue sky puffed white with clouds. She scrutinized the bird's wingspan and watched its beady black eyes scouring the water, *searching*, marking its shadow on the river.

Reclining against Julian, she wondered if she should fear the creature, but in the canoe her husband and other officers propelled the craft forward, driving their paddles into a difficult flow, struggling upstream, seemingly unaware.

"It's a bad omen," she heard Mack say. "The eagle is a sacred bird; it comes with a warning."

Sitting at the canoe's bow the past two days, the tracker had assisted them on their journey south. Alert, quiet and contemplative, and ever watchful, his presence gave Madeleine a measure of comfort and distress at the same time.

"Do not worry me with your negativity," Julian said, propelling the canoe closer to shore. "It's a bird of prey hunting for fish, Mack, and nothing more."

"Its presence on the river should alert your notice."

"I see your sour look, but I do not believe in such things as aboriginal legends."

"The 'Great Spirit,'" Mack replied, still studying the bird, "deserves some respect. Disregard the warning if you must. Kiah would travel north, heading for…"

"Safer shores? Return to Ville de Québec? I don't have the luxury of retreat. I have my orders."

"Kiah has told me the stories of her people and shared the spirit signs in our travels. The eagle's shrill cry, the wind's whistle, the spirit bear waiting on the shore. I have no reason to believe; I was not born of the same spirit religion. Still, a man understands worry when he hears its wobble in his wife's voice, which tells me I should listen in times like this. And be wary. Alert. Watchful."

"I watch for more obvious signs," Julian said, glancing at the eagle. "No more talk of omens or concerns we cannot see with our own eyes. I shall not frighten the officers or the women with aboriginal tales. Do you understand?"

"You're a hard ass, Captain," Mack said, dipping his

paddle in the water and stroking calmly. "Many have lost their lives with less subtle signs."

"Julian, is there something to fear?" Madeleine asked, her forehead furrowing.

He didn't answer straight away.

"We're not in Ville de Québec any longer," Mack replied, looking toward the shore. "We're traveling a waterway once known as the Iroquois River. We'd like to think this is our land, *our river*, however, the Iroquois warriors feel we're trespassing on ground that belongs to them. Threatening their villages, threatening their way of life."

"Endangering the supply chain, you mean. So threatened, they side with the British and raid our colony, our…"

"People." Madeleine finished, worrying.

They paddled to the shore. Once they arrived at the bank's edge, Julian left the canoe in a hurry. "I'm sorry, Madeleine," he said, coming to her, taking her hand and assisting her from the canoe to the rocky shore. "Mack understands the aboriginal history in these parts, but perhaps his information is better left unsaid."

"Mack meant no harm."

"It's not a fair game to usher in this talk of fear," Julian said, staring at his friend and giving him a warning to be silent. "We cannot concern ourselves with the unknown. Let's consider the labors ahead as we portage across the land. The journey will be difficult."

Madeleine didn't move. She stood helpless on the shoreline, contemplating what Mack had said about trespassing, realizing she stood on sacred ground beside an

Iroquois waterway. She watched Julian assisting his men as they retrieved three canoes from swiftly flowing waters. "Will we be safe?"

"Your question is without merit. An officer does not dwell on uncertainty."

"But Mack said… Surely his insight should give rise to caution."

"Nonsense. Mack should have kept his omens and aboriginal history to himself. We'll won't talk anymore about myths."

"What will we talk about then? The beautiful sky, the trees, the screeching birdsong in the air?"

Julian snickered and left his men to their work to seek Madeleine where she stood. "Fear is an emotion I won't hold, and neither should you concern yourself with such anxieties." He stepped to her, clutched her face in his hand. "The eagle is also a sign of courage. Mack knows this. Take a deep breath, Madeleine, let your worries go. I'm aware of the troubles, both present and past. Breathe the fresh air, enjoy this moment, and every moment until we breathe our last breath."

"My last breath? Julian, your words do little to stem my fears."

He released his grip. "Put your mind at ease and leave the strategic demands to your captain. You're about to receive a rest from sitting inside an uncomfortable canoe, you'll naught sit in the craft for a few hours. Enjoy the break and the walk through the forest. But my men," he snorted, his hands on his hips, "for them, a heavy trek lies ahead." He motioned with his hands. "We have to carry our gear and it's at least a day's walk to reach our destination."

An officer made a face while grasping a pack from the canoe. "A bitch's load," he grunted, placing the pack's burden on his back. "And one a woman such as you would never want to carry."

Madeleine pondered the statement of physical weight. She wisely remained silent as she had her own burdens to carry, such as the unborn child who continually kicked beneath her breastbone. She leaned backward, aching from the journey. Oh yes, a woman carried her own weight, burdens a man, being male, could never comprehend.

The canoe was soon emptied and upturned with three men carrying its weight above their heads, and three more carrying the cargo. The group proceeded upstream, walking south along the river.

"The path appears undisturbed," Mack said, peering at the ground intently, tracking upriver. "Not so much as a bent blade of grass."

"Doesn't mean anything," Julian replied, scrutinizing the trail. "Iroquois tactics include stalking the officers like you'd court a fine woman. They lie in wait, rushing their prey from the bushes, shock and awe, inflicting as much hurt and pain as possible, and then retreating back into the bush. That's the style of warfare they favor."

"True enough," Mack said, continuing along the trail, his sword arm at the ready.

"Madeleine…"

She turned to the sound of Julian's voice, and he approached her carrying a musket, an ever-present serious expression pinching his face. "It's heavy," he said, placing the musket in her hands. But he didn't release the weapon. "Can you carry it?"

"It's no great burden. I can manage it."

He simply nodded. "Mack, I want you to take the lead at the front of the line."

"Oh thanks," he guffawed, moving into place.

"Gauvain, your crew will follow Mack."

"As you will, Captain."

"Jacques, pull up the rear and I will take the center. Are we ready, men?"

"Yes, sir." Someone grunted.

"Then we walk."

They trudged upstream, following a well-trodden hard-packed trail. Madeleine imagined the forest creatures, deer maybe, that had walked this path. Perhaps native people, too.

She became aware of the weight pinching at her shoulders from the musket strap and the bags she had to carry. Powder to prime the chamber. Powder to pour inside the muzzle. Carrying the musket and bearing its weight, she reflected on the instructions.

Grasp the cartridge; bite the paper from the load, spit, then load the muzzle...

The birdsong became infrequent. Did she hear a branch break? *Crack.* She studied the emerald-green shrubbery, scrutinizing large deciduous trees that men could easily crouch behind.

Just the wind whispering and my own overactive imagination.

After walking a distance, the drone of water flowing over

large gray boulders became more pronounced, masking the sound of their footsteps. Tired, Madeleine paused to take in water-washed limestone, wishing they could stop and rest, but grateful she didn't suffer the weight of a large canoe or burdensome packs. The men bore the strain, exhibiting pinched expressions while a warm sun beaded against her face.

"Keep walking," Julian ordered, coming beside her. "We must reach the fort before nightfall."

A soft padding of feet caught her attention, followed by the sound of branches snapping. A tweak so slight, she thought her mind was playing tricks. Madeleine turned to the noise but saw nothing.

"Drop your burdens and load your weapons." Julian shouted orders, drawing his musket, leaving his sword slung at his waist. "They come."

Madeleine scanned the area to see why Julian had given the order, searching beyond the tree line. At first, she didn't see much.

"Take to your arms," he screamed, stepping closer to her. "Load your muskets!"

Not far away, a half-dressed man raced through the trees, coming closer to her. Agile, he sprinted over a bush like a buck, running, leaping over smaller shrubbery with ease.

Taking a step backward, Madeleine watched him come, scrutinizing a face painted blood red with streaks of ashen black across his cheeks.

"Load your weapon!" Julian screamed as he fired. "Madeleine…"

The warrior fell… but other men raced closer, weapons in their hands. *What were they holding in their hands?*

"Fire," Julian yelled, pushing her behind him. "Now!"

Frightened, Madeleine jumped when the first volley of muskets exploded, shattering the peace. As smoke drifted into the air, she could not tell how many warriors rushed toward them. The braves seemed to charge from different directions, enclosing them, especially as they encountered the other officers.

"Reload!"

The order sparked Madeleine to action. *Stay calm*, she told herself, but she heard a woman screaming, Julian shouting orders, and all the while her hands shook as she retrieved the cartridge, soon pouring black powder into the muzzle. She was still tamping her load when a second volley fired. A warrior breached her safety. She screamed, shrinking backward when he reached for her hair, yanking her backward, but she held her weapon, knowing she had to put powder in the pan.

Julian didn't say a word as he rushed toward her, his arm raised, his sword at the ready, charging the warrior and slashing him across the belly.

"Stay behind me!" Julian screamed; his movements were jerky, stepping this way and that, "and for hell's sake, load your weapon!"

Nodding—*shaking*—her heart pounding, Madeleine primed the pan, then raised her musket as more warriors raced from the trees.

Boom! The weapon discharged, causing her to flinch, and delivering a white puff of spray in the air. *Did I hit anyone?*

She had missed her target. No time to reload the gun. Painted hands carrying tomahawks grabbed at her. Dug into her waist, yanked at her hair, pulling at her, trying to lead her away.

She screamed…

"Stay close," Julian yelled, wrenching her to his side, swinging his sword, metal slicing through a belly, spurting red, cutting an arm, slashing left and right, and the spray of more red blood.

A hand grasped her waist, squeezing, trying to pull her away. She screamed, fighting, squirming. Searching for courage, she butted her musket against the barbarian's forehead. Fear turned to a need to survive.

A shot let off and Julian's hold released. Marie appeared at her side. "Okay?" she asked, her expression frightened, looking left and right.

"Load your weapon. Again!" Julian screamed, sticking his assailant with his sword.

Madeleine reached for a cartridge, her fingers quivering, the spray of something wet against her face. She ignored the resultant cry, biting the paper from the cartridge. She tamped the load and primed the pan. A hand grabbed her hair and yanked. *Not this time*! She spun around, seeing the hateful expression of a warrior.

Boom. She fired the musket; standing so close to the warrior she witnessed his startled expression, watched the blood seep from a gaping wound in his chest. The warrior collapsed to the ground.

She loaded the musket, twisting left, then right, hearing the boom of other muskets firing, then spinning in time to see Julian struck by an arrow in his arm, his forehead bleeding. *Bleeding!* A brave rushed nearer.

"Julian…" she screamed, horrified.

A shot rang out and thick gray-white smoke filled the air. The Aboriginal brave who would have scalped the hair from her husband's head, fell to the ground.

"You owe me, Benoit," Mack said, raising his musket again and firing. "The bastards, they're retreating now."

"Someone needs to hold the line."

"Fire," Marie screamed. Madeleine took out another threat. She loaded her weapon again, waiting for the next attack, but the remaining warriors ran the way they had come, returning to the forest.

"Julian…" Madeleine cried, dropping the musket and falling to her knees at his side where he lay on the ground. "Tell me you're all right." Marie reloaded her weapon and stood guard over them.

"I'm…"

"Doctor," Mack shouted, "the captain's in need of your attention."

Madeleine grasped his arm, seeing the arrow through his flesh. Blood seeped from his right arm, spilling to the ground and an ugly gash had split the skin at his forehead wide. So much red…

"You're hurt," Madeleine said, grasping his arm. "Please someone, help him."

Marie stood above her, still holding her musket, wearing a horrified expression on her face. "I cannot see Gauvain," she said, her voice breaking. Holding her musket, she spun left, then right, searching. "He's not here. Could they have taken him?"

Jacques pressed close. "Move aside, ladies. Mack, let me help the captain."

Madeleine did as he requested, feeling helpless. "Is it grave?"

"Give me a strip of your skirt."

"Mrs. Benoit," he yelled, "I need the cloth, now—And someone, please search for my wife!"

Geneviève? Where was Geneviève? Madeleine reached for the hem of her skirt, tearing until a wide swath of fabric came free. She passed it to Jacques.

"Another."

She ripped another square of cloth and passed it over.

Several minutes passed, but it appeared the attack was over. Now that it appeared safe, Madeleine knelt beside her husband.

"Maddie," he whispered, reaching for her hand, "are you hurt?"

"I'm…, I'm fine," she stuttered, her voice quivering, tears leaking from her eyes. "But you're not."

"The surgeon," he winced, "will see to my wounds."

"The surgeon?"

"Did you think I would travel south with an expectant wife, and no one to deliver our child?"

"Our child?" she whispered, massaging his arm. "You would think of the baby when you're hurt, lying here on the ground?"

"Of course," he said, his eyes dazed, confused.

The surgeon smacked his face. "You're all right, Captain Benoit. Someone, bring me a blanket."

His eyes fluttered as he gazed at her. "Maddie—"

She grasped his hand and squeezed. "You must not leave me, Julian Benoit. I crossed an ocean to find you."

"A turbulent sea you've found, ma chérie. Have no fear; I'm tired, wounded… But I will not leave you."

CHAPTER 27

*M*adeleine carried her musket the grueling distance to Fort Sainte-Anne, managing a strength she hadn't known she possessed. Even when her arms ached, *tortured by the iron*, somehow, she bore the weapon's weight. Stumbling on occasion, anxiety twisting in her gut, and constantly on the verge of illness, she promised herself should trouble come again, she would not flinch when preparing or firing the weapon.

Guilt. Worry. She had immigrated to a country occupied by a savage nation. The aboriginal warriors had dispensed their menace, but their group had been fortunate. No further attacks had occurred on their journey south.

Now situated in a small bedchamber with Julian, she sat in an armchair beside his sick bed, staring at her husband. He suffered moments of unconsciousness, opening his eyes, moaning in pain, then succumbing to sleep again while she waited for him to become more alert.

She stroked his bandaged forehead, ensured he was

comfortable in the bed, and tucked his injured arm under the coverlets. Listening to his breathing, she thought the room oppressive without his voice. The lack of conversation was her fault. If she had not flinched, had loaded her weapon sooner as her husband had commanded, he might not have been hurt. Julian had been forced to protect his wife—

"It's not your fault," Marie whispered, placing her hand on Madeleine's shoulder where she sat on the bed.

"Of course, it is. Look at him—" Madeleine moaned, her lower lip trembling, "—silent in this bed. Unconscious. If I hadn't been such a simpleton; such a ninny, if I had listened to his instructions and obeyed them to the letter."

"You're not an officer. Madeleine, you're being too hard on yourself. He's alive and there's every hope he'll recover."

Madeleine twisted on the mattress, turning to Marie, seeing her friend's equally grave expression. "I'm sorry, Marie. I should be more sympathetic to you, given your situation. The officers will find Gauvain."

She shook her head. "They've searched the forest. There's no sign of him. No sign of Geneviève either. They have been taken, taken by those barbarians. Mack will not tell me what they will do to them."

"Perhaps, it's best," Madeleine said, swallowing, "not to know. They might harm a man. Do you think they would harm a woman?"

"Yes, I think they might."

"Terrible. Poor Geneviève, so young and beautiful. Life is cruel and unfair."

"I didn't love him," Marie screeched, turning away from her friend, her voice breaking. "We were simply…"

"Of course," Madeleine said, rising to her feet. "You knew him but a moment."

"I could tell he was a womanizer," she cried out; tears threatening, she turned away. "I understood his natural inclinations from the start. Perhaps, it's best?"

"Oh Marie, you don't mean to say such unkind sentiments."

"I accepted Gauvain into my life for better or for worse. I hoped for the better, hoped his cheeky tendencies would change in time. This cannot be happening," she said, wiping a tear from her face. "I wanted a husband, just like you, but for reasons different than your own. *To have and to hold.* I came so far to find him, a man who could give me a better life. And those cruel beings, they have taken him."

"I'm sorry," Madeleine said, stepping closer, placing her hand on Marie's shoulder. What good would her regard do? What could she say that would make a difference?

"Where do I go now? What do I do, without him?"

"We will take care of you," Julian lamented from his bed. "Don't worry, Marie."

"Julian," Madeleine blurted, turning to her husband, placing her hand against his chest. "You're awake."

"I'm glad to see you more alert, Captain." Marie sighed, stepping away. "It's about time. I'll take my leave. I need to be alone, to consider my options."

Julian nodded. Madeleine watched Marie trudge toward the door, grasp the handle and retreat from the room. Her heart ached for her friend, but what could she do that might make the situation better? Nothing. Not even friendship could mend a hole in the human heart.

JULIAN LAY on the bed scrutinizing her expression. Silent. Staring. The perusal made Madeleine uncomfortable. Sitting on the armchair beside his bed, she gazed at her mulberry gown.

"Do not look at me with wanting in your eyes," she whispered, gazing away, clasping her hands in her lap. "Talk to me, Julian. What concern wrinkles your brow?"

Dressed in a white lawn shirt and brown breeches, he lifted his free hand to his forehead. "My head is hurting. I wish I'd listened to Mack when he mentioned the eagle. A natural omen? I'm a fool for not heeding his advice."

Madeleine breathed a sigh of relief. His attention was not on his wife and her perceived responsibility for his wounds. "Just rest," she said, stretching forward and placing her hand on his shoulder. "The horror is past. No need to dwell on what we cannot change."

"How long have I lain here?"

"Not long. We only arrived at Fort Sainte-Anne this past evening."

"I don't recall arriving. I don't remember much at all, not since the…"

"Attack?" Madeleine said, finishing his comment. "You sustained a blow to your forehead. The wound was awful. It was difficult watching Jacques place the stitches."

"Not nearly as troublesome as the wallop, let me assure you. I'm still seeing stars."

"I'm sorry. This is my fault."

"Hmm," he muttered, raising his fingers to the injury, his

fingers sliding across the bandaging. "Oh, I see. 'Twas my wife who raised a blade against her husband's head?"

"I should have loaded the musket sooner."

Madeleine waited for Julian to respond. She bit at the corner of her lip while he scrutinized her face as if he had never studied her facial features before. Surprisingly, he reached for her. She closed her eyes as his fingertips drifted along the edge of her cheek, causing shivers to ripple down her spine.

"I'd rather have suffered an injury, than see my wife hurt, taken—or worse—slain."

"I tremble while contemplating their plight. Poor Gauvain and Geneviève. No sign of them. What's happening to them, and will they be found?"

"We can best hope the Mohawk people will hold them for ransom."

"Would they kill Gauvain? Would they hurt a woman?"

"I think you know the answer to that, Madeleine."

"Aw, poor Marie," she sighed, glancing away. "Jacques, too."

"Come," he said meaningfully, "lie beside me."

"Do you think that's a wise idea? You're hurt."

Julian winced noticeably as he shifted, making a space for her. "I'm not dead," he scowled, patting the bedding. "I want to hold my wife."

She did as he requested, shifting layers of skirts, and lying stiffly beside him. If he sensed her unease, he pretended not to notice.

"Put your head on my shoulder."

She rolled to her right side, surrendering to him. He

nudged her waist, pulling her closer. She swallowed; he kissed her forehead, grasped her right hand and held her fingers against his chest.

"Madeleine, we've been husband and wife for over a month now. Do you think we might?"

She knew what he meant but it surprised her that he broached the subject now. "Julian, you're hurt."

He urged her hand lower. She nibbled at her lip when her palm touched his waist. "Do not change the subject. It's time to consummate this marriage, don't you think?"

Pulling away from his grasp, she rose onto her elbow to stare at his hazel eyes, seeing his need. "What do you see when you look at me, Julian? Why do you want me so? I'm no more than a…"

"Ah," he snickered, smiling, retrieving her hand. "I know you. I've studied you when you didn't know I was looking. You've walked beside me, not expecting anything more than my support. One smile makes me dizzy, weak at the knees. You're beautiful, inside and out."

She gazed at his chest, her fingers drawing imaginary circles on the flaxen fabric. "That's kind of you to say, I never thought I'd hear such a depiction, though I do not deserve your sensitivity."

"What do I deserve?" he asked, grasping her hand and placing it on his erection. A firm penis lay beneath her hand, hidden inside his breeches. She cupped him gently, hearing him groan in response. "I want to be with you, mine wife."

"Even though you will not be my first?"

"I may not be your second, or even your third."

Madeleine gasped, released her hold and rose to a sitting position. "Julian…"

"Do not deny it," he said with a grimace, pulling her back to him. "No more secrets between us."

Ashamed, Madeleine tried to pull away, but Julian would not release his hold. She scrutinized his face, seeing understanding, heat and passion, too. "Some truths are not easy to share. I wanted to bury my ugliness. Wash myself clean. Start anew."

"The father of your child, do you know his name?"

She swallowed, not knowing what to say. Staring at her husband, tears filled her eyes and threatened to slip free. "There was more than one man," she admitted, shaking her head.

She stared at her husband, waiting for his damning response. The moments lingered, but he didn't say anything, so she tried to explain.

"I have not lied to you, Julian. I gave away a piece of my soul to repay a gambling debt owed to my father. I lost a second chunk to the very next man, to secure a meal. I was hungry… and once you've sold yourself twice, someone else's pleasure feeds your debt."

"I know." He nodded, pulling her into his arms. "Let me reclaim your soul. Restore your lost spirit. Let me love you, Madeleine. Let me be the husband you sought across the ocean, a father for your child."

"Julian?" Madeleine whispered, tears slipping from her eyes, disbelieving of his kindness. "Do you mean what you say?"

"Ma chérie," he said, threading his fingers in her chestnut

hair, pulling her to his lips. "Tell me you want me. I seek a price as well, but I'll return the favor with my heart. I'll not force you to love me."

So close to his lips, yet she paused to stare at their fullness, and the heated measure of his observation. Need lingered in his hazel eyes, and she was hungry for something more than exploitation. Taking a chance at a future together, she kissed him. "Are you sure? You're hurt."

"I'm hurting… lower, and I'm dying for release."

She contemplated an unladylike act. "I'm quite heavy with child. My large belly will not upset you?"

"You're radiant. Beautiful."

Madeleine giggled, shaking her head. "All right. I want our first occasion to be pleasurable, but given the urgency…"

"And the fact I could succumb to unconsciousness again, soon."

"A ploy, Julian, and you know it, too."

"You've kept me waiting."

"Not for much longer."

Madeleine took a deep breath. She could do this. He was her husband after all. Sitting beside Julian, she pulled up his shirt, grasped the belt at his waist and undid the buckle.

"Pretend it's your first time, wife. That I'm the only man you've ever hungered for. The only man you've ever taken to your bed."

The leather slid between her fingers, she stared at the bulge beneath the woolen fabric. His need was obvious. The tingling sensation in her gut mirrored his need. The realization was sudden and inexplicable. She wanted her husband, too. She threw the belt on the floor.

"You are the 'only' man, Julian, I have wanted this way."

"Do you mean it?" he asked, moaning as she undid his buttons, slowly, one at a time.

Parting the folds of brown fabric, she gazed at his manliness. "You're beautiful," Madeleine sighed, untying the garters beneath his knees. "I've never wanted to give a man anything more in my life. I will make you happy. Raise your bottom so I can remove the barrier."

He rose and Madeleine slipped off his breeches, sliding the garment along strong lean legs. She threw them to the floor, pausing to stare at her husband. He smiled. She heaved layers of skirt around her waist and then climbed Julian's legs, meeting his erection. Lounging above him, his shaft touching her moist skin, she felt no shame in the contact as in times past. Yet she paused, holding back.

Julian slipped his hands underneath her skirt, his fingers climbing her stockings, rising above her thighs. She shivered when he grasped her waist with both hands. "If there's any comfort in this first joining, you'll feel no pain."

"There's that."

"May I, mine wife, fit myself inside?"

Although unsure, she nodded, staring at his eyes. He shifted beneath her satin skin, stroking her mound, nudging his manhood against her folds. She closed her eyes, squeezing them shut tight, thinking he'd ask her to ride him like a man rode a horse. It was her only experience, her only knowledge of the act. She didn't know what to do so waited for his instruction.

He pressed upward. Madeleine felt the stroke, heard his

groan, saw his answering wince. Anxiety at their sex-play immediately turned to concern for her husband.

"Julian, should we stop?"

"No," he replied, wincing, touching his bandaged forehead. "But you'll have to take your own pleasure. My head hurts when I move too much."

"Take my pleasure? What do you mean?"

He didn't say anything for the space of several seconds. Madeleine worried she had acted improperly.

"Have you never received equal measure, your own satisfaction?"

"I don't understand. Have I done something wrong?"

"You've done nothing to warrant concern, but in our first engagement as man and wife, you will have your pleasure first. I insist on it. Come, lie beside me."

Unsure, Madeleine did as her husband asked, soon lying on the bed. He climbed above her. His breath was ragged as he sought the underpinnings from her gown. He removed them, placing them on the bureau. He tackled the laces to her stays, opening the garment wide. She didn't grumble when together they exited the bed and he assisted her to remove both garments. She soon stood before her husband wearing only her shift.

"You're beautiful, my chérie. It's true."

"I'm nothing of the sort."

"Oh," he whispered, cupping linen-covered breasts, "but you are, exquisite."

He grasped the shift and assisted in removing the garment, pulling it over her head. He smiled, contemplating her breasts as if they were a work of art. She moaned when he grasped her left breast, soon suckling the other.

"Julian—" She gasped, arching her back, "what are you doing to me?"

"Preparing a path for our love."

She didn't know how he managed it, but his fingers soon danced at her entrance. "I can tell you want me."

"How do you know?"

"Your folds are wet. I would bathe them with my tongue if we were not standing."

Madeleine had believed this type of sexuality was wrong, but this man was her husband, and the fingers stroking her sensitive folds filled her with erotic need. She arched against him, enjoying each stroke, finding pleasure in his mouth suckling her nipple.

"Julian, surely this is wrong?" she asked, panting. Weak in the knees, she collapsed on the bed. But her husband followed her to the edge, his fingers stroking, reaching inside.

Something overcame her, a feeling she'd never experienced before. "Julian," she cried out, gasping with the orgasm.

"Have you felt it?" he asked, his eyes alight with wonder, staring into her eyes.

"Yes."

"Slide backward, my love."

She nodded, scaling the counterpane, her legs sliding apart. He fitted himself between her thighs.

"May I?" he asked. She nodded, *yes*.

Her husband drew himself inside of her, holding himself still, gazing at her face as if to question if this melding of bodies was appropriate. She leaned backward, spreading her legs wider, grasping his bare bottom with her hands. He began an exercise, a rhythm as old as time. She wondered at his gentleness, the ease and exit of entry, filling her with the expertise of a landed gentry. She held his shoulders, watching a serious expression wrinkle his face.

She knew the moment when he found his own release, for he buried the hilt of his shaft and then held still. "Madeleine…" He breathed her name. He stared at her, appearing thoughtful but not retreating from the lap of physical enjoyment he had found.

"What is it?"

"Oh, my dearest, I love you, Madeleine Bourbonnais, if this is your real name."

"Of course." She smiled, sighing with relief. "I've carried it my entire life, at least until I became your wife. But what did you say to me?"

He reclined to her side, pulling her close. "I'll never give myself to another. I'll love you until the day I die."

She grasped his cheek, smiling, thinking she might cry. "How could I have been so fortunate to find you, a heart across the ocean, a husband I have come to love, too!"

"Say it, ma chérie. Proclaim it."

"Will it cost me?"

"Madeleine…"

"Oh, very well, it costs me nothing to share the truth. I chose you from the start. I love you, Julian. I thank you for all you have given. For me and for…"

"Our child," he said, placing his hand on her belly. The baby moved in response. "When will our son arrive?"

"It could be a girl?"

"Oh no, this baby is a boy, a strong lad to assist his father with the management of our land. I'll need sons to mind the farm."

"I'll help you."

"You'll be busy in the kitchen, or busy in the..."

"Bedchamber? Only if you give me further, ah, pleasure."

"Pleasure," he chuckled, pressing against her. "I'm always open to giving and receiving."

"Would you consider another, ah, pleasurable session?"

"My head is weak with the idea, but..."

"Oh Julian," Madeleine giggled as his fingers found her sensitive tissues, "the baby is protesting your advance..."

CHAPTER 28

*J*ulian had to tell Madeleine about his mission. He was not afraid to accept his duty, to travel into Iroquois territory and seek the Mohawk Nation in battle, but there were reasons to defy his orders and they included *his wife*. The first company was deploying on Wednesday. He didn't want to leave. He'd not soon forget the tenderness discovered in her embrace. How could he leave his wife now, when she had finally accepted his heart into her hands?

"What's wrong, Julian?"

He smiled in response to Madeleine's question, perusing her sleep-tousled expression. Lying beside him in their bed, he loved her warm breath feathering against his chest, her fingers stroking his skin beneath his shirt. "You're perceptive. I have kept news of my mission from you."

"Oh?" she cooed, glancing away. "Will you tell me?"

Pouting, she reached upward, her index finger slid across his forehead.

"I don't want to tell you anything," he chuckled, smiling too, "to tell you the truth, but some secrets cannot be kept forever."

"We traveled to Fort Sainte-Anne for a reason, and given the attack on your officers, on our group, I knew the time would come when a war might be waged."

"The Iroquois people are dangerous."

"I understand their stealth. I'm still having nightmares."

"I wish I did not have to go. I don't want this fight, this mission, but they refuse to come to the peace table, and as you've seen, offer their savagery, ambushing our people. There's no other option but to meet them on the field of battle. I wish it were otherwise."

"I was worried you might have to leave, but your wounds are only starting to heal. Surely, you won't go?"

"I must lead my men into battle."

"Of course, but…"

"The first company leaves on Wednesday. I've convinced the commander to let my men leave on Friday."

Madeleine clutched his shirtfront, nestled her head beneath his chin, clinging to him like a child. "Please, you cannot leave me, Julian."

He pulled her close. "I understand your fears, but I will return to you."

"Losing you, I could not bear it."

"Ah chérie, I see the worry in your eyes, the love shining there. I will return. I hate to boast, but I'm good at what I do."

"Your head begs to differ."

"It's healing well, I think."

"A thin red line. The doctor stitched it well."

"Ah, Jacques," he said meaningfully, kissing her forehead. "I chose him to accompany us on our journey. He'll assist you when you go into labor. Should something happen…"

She pressed closer, touching his neck, her fingers wandering into the loose strands of his hair. He was tempted to take advantage.

"Don't say it. I could not bear it if you didn't return. You're my family; the only one I can depend on."

"But we must talk. If something were to happen…"

"Don't say it. I refuse to think bad thoughts."

Julian stretched backward so he could see his wife's face. Her forehead wrinkled with worry, her eyes shone with unshed tears. This fear, he didn't like it any better than she, but he went into battle with a plan. His wife would have a plan, too.

"If the worst should happen, you're to return to France and seek the Benoit family. They will take care of you."

"Carrying a child that doesn't hold your bloodline?" she said with a grimace. "They would never accept me."

"You're my wife. You carry my child."

"You're a generous man, but it's not true. Perhaps it would be better to stay in Canada, find another husband."

"No way," he said with a smirk, pulling her to his chest. "I will not have another man hold what is mine."

"Then no more on this subject. Come back to me."

"I will," he stated, seeking her lips, nibbling. "It's part of my plan, but for now let me love you. I need to hold you…"

"God would be cruel to steal my—"

"No more talk. Love me, Madeleine."

She was losing her shyness. Her fingers wandered across his chest, tracing the indentation between his ribs; higher, lower, evoking his physical need. In return he massaged her breasts, her belly, feeling the swell, unafraid of what lay inside.

Julian had made so many promises in his life, but this one he meant to keep. Love was worth the fight!

THREE DAYS LATER, Julian's company deployed. Standing beside Marie, Madeleine watched her husband and a column of men marching toward the front gates of Fort Sainte-Anne. She had hoped to escape sensibilities of the heart, by concealing her emotions to support her husband. But her sentiments rose to the surface anyway, constricting her breathing. Tears filled her eyes and slid down her cheeks. She dashed the wetness away, hoping Julian would not notice. He had to leave. He needed to be strong to face the difficulties ahead.

He paused in his pursuit and looked back; their eyes made contact. He stood apart from his officers. Glimpsing her sorrow, he soon rushed to her side.

He grasped her face with both hands and stared into her eyes. "I will return," he said forcefully. "You have my word."

"Your men are watching us, Julian."

"They will have my command shortly. I don't care who witnesses my compassion, or my love for you. Let the entire fort take notice of our moment," he said, kissing her firmly on the lips, "after all, you're my wife and my primary concern.

My heart constricts seeing your pain, seeing your tears. I don't want to leave you."

"But you must take your leave," Madeleine said, blinking, choking on her words.

"When I'm ready, I'll go." He wiped the liquid away with his finger. "But not without one last kiss, one last hug, to take with me where I go."

Julian pulled her close. She closed her eyes while holding him, lounging against his chest, breathing his masculine scent, loving his arms, his strength, sighing when his hand clutched her derriere.

"You grasped me in front of your men; I cannot believe you did that," she whispered in his ear, taking a deep inhalation of air.

"I'll be back," he said, releasing her, stepping away. She felt cold without him near.

"Marie, please take care of my wife while I'm away. Life is harder at the fort. She needs to be mindful of her activities."

"I'll keep Maddie entertained," Marie promised.

"One more thing, Marie…"

"Yes?"

"If the truth can be learned of Gauvain or Geneviève, I will discover what happened to them."

Marie simply nodded, gazing at the ground.

"I won't say goodbye," Julian said, gripping Madeleine's shoulders, kissing her lips one final time.

"I love you," Madeleine replied, her eyes wet. "Be safe, Julian."

"Je t'aime aussi."

He left her then, emotion shining in his eyes.

Approaching his officers, he studied her intently, but then shouted orders to his officers to leave. The gates opened and a column of men marched through the threshold, leaving Madeleine and Fort Sainte-Anne behind.

She had never felt so bereft or alone. A cold wind blew against her face, the fabric of her gown swirled around her legs. Julian nodded one final time, and then he was gone.

Come back to me, Julian.

CHAPTER 29

A wall of round timbers squared the perimeter of Fort Sainte-Anne, standing six to eight feet tall. The walls blocked the sun in the morning and late in the day, so Madeleine took her walks at noonday when the sun was highest in the sky. The walls were tall and foreboding and Madeleine should have felt safe within the fortification, but regardless of the walls' height, she missed the company of her husband. If he were here, she'd feel safer.

"You miss him," Marie said, accompanying her on the walk.

"Every passing day, I think of him. I hope he's safe, but there's been no word, at least not to my knowledge."

"Only a week has passed."

"He could already be in combat, could already be…"

"Do not think ill-thoughts," Marie said, grasping her shoulder. "I'm sure he's safe."

Madeleine paused, straining to see through the logs, but they were packed so tightly together, she could barely see through the cracks. "I wish he would return. Seems like we've only found each other."

"I've noticed the way you smile when you speak of Julian. Does this mean there's hope for the two of you? And, have you found love in this new world, despite your condition?"

Madeleine smiled, pausing to take in her friend's observation. "Is it obvious?"

"You're glowing, but your light has always come from within; perhaps your condition assists, too?"

Madeleine started to walk again. "He's accepted the child. Has promised to be a father when the baby's born."

"Warms my heart to know good men can still be found."

"Oh, Marie," Madeleine said, pausing, "I see your crestfallen face. I'm sorry for your loss. Maybe Julian will bring good news when the regiment returns. Maybe Gauvain will be found."

"I haven't given up hope. Until there's a body, or some time has passed, I will not consider his death."

"You must not worry."

"Travelers at the front gates," the guard called out. Madeleine turned to the sound, but whoever had journeyed to the fort, they were still too far away to see.

"A pity," she said, gazing at Marie. "They're not our officers."

"How many rounds do you intend to walk today? Perhaps it's time for a break, or a cup of tea?"

Madeleine shrugged. "How will you survive the winter? We've not been outside all that long."

"It's cold today, Madeleine. Doesn't the wind hurt your face?"

"I feel the cold as much as the next person, but I cannot sit around thinking, or be trapped inside my quarters. I need to keep busy. Feel productive. I'll go crazy if I stay in that small room."

"I'll keep you distracted. Let's go inside. Perhaps we could do some sewing? Practice with our needles and thread?"

"Ha!" Madeleine laughed, amused. "Darning and all manner of stitchery is *not* one of my best skills. But we don't need more excuses. Let's go inside."

SOMEONE KNOCKED at the bedchamber door. Sitting beside a small wooden table, Madeleine placed her teacup on the side plate and glanced at the door. Marie did the same.

"Come in," she exclaimed, shifting on her seat.

A lower-ranking officer poked his head in the room. "Mademoiselle Benoit, I'm sorry to disturb your luncheon, but a gentleman has come to the fort, and he insists on your company."

"Who is this man?" she asked, worrying. "Does he have a name?"

"Jean," a familiar voice remarked. The gent pushed past the officer and forced his way inside her room. Shocked to see her brother, Madeleine's heart nearly stopped. No stranger to her, a ruggedly handsome man paused in the middle of the room. Sporting a full beard and wearing tan leather clothing, he might have passed for a fur trapper, but this man, her brother, she'd know his face anywhere.

"Jean," Madeleine screeched. She pushed away from the table and rose from the chair. She hurried across the space to meet him but stopped, seeing a look of shock marring her brother's expression. He scrutinized her overly large stomach and seemed shocked at seeing her belly. Shame filled her momentarily, but she squashed the feeling, took a breath, and gathered her courage.

Collecting himself, he breached the distance between them and grasped her hands, appearing like he might cry. He pulled her into his embrace. She could feel her enlarged belly resting against his abdomen. "Madeleine, I've found you, finally, but…"

"This is a surprise to me, too. I've so much to tell you."

He stepped away but did not release her hands. "You've been in my thoughts for weeks. I returned home to France and found our family home had been sold. Our parents dead, and you…missing."

"I thought you were dead," Madeleine began, tears of joy pooling in her eyes. "Dead and buried at sea. But here you are, standing close to me. How did you find me?"

"Heaven only knows," he said with a grimace. A whoosh of air expelled from his chest. "I thought I'd never see you again. For a time, I thought you must be dead. I tried not to lose hope. I didn't know what to do, whom to turn to, or where to look. I called on everyone I could think of, our father's gambling buddies—creditors as well."

Madeleine freed his hand and stepped away from him, turning, facing Marie. "My brother," she explained.

"After learning you had become an orphan on the street…"

"It's all right, Jean. I'm aware of my past, you may continue your story."

"I learned of your travel to New France when I questioned a night watchman, and soon after, the Captain of the Saint-Jean Baptiste. My God, so many weeks at sea to find you, hoping to prevent the eventuality of a forced husband. Why, Madeleine? Why did you do it? Sail to this miserable land?"

"Ahem," Marie interrupted, rising from her chair. "I should leave, permit brother and sister to get reacquainted, privately."

"I don't think so," Madeleine replied. "Whatever Jean has to say to me, or I to him, you're free to hear the conversation. Now where were we, Jean. You want to know why I'm in Canada? Why I've sailed to this new world?"

"You came as a ward of the king. You did it then, you married an officer."

"I'm married. I've chosen well. My husband is a captain."

"He cannot possibly be the father," Jean said with a wince, motioning to her belly. "For the love of God, you're with child. Who shamed you? I'll hunt him down; he'll wish he'd never sullied your good name."

"Believe me, if you could challenge the man who wronged me, and force him to pay for his crime, I would be grateful, but it's too late for justice. And you'll have to sail to France if you want to deliver on such a promise."

"I should leave," Marie stated, walking to the door.

"No!" Madeleine said forcefully, grasping her hand. "You won't leave."

"Well, if I'm going to stay, perhaps proper introductions

are in order? Monsieur Bourbonnais, I'm Marie Chauvet, Madeleine's dearest friend. Let me say, I see your shock at learning your sister's condition, but she has been through much while you've been sailing, seeing the riches of the Orient, perhaps, while living the life of a merchant. Be warned. Brother or not, please be kind to my friend, or you'll have to answer to me."

"An honor to meet you, Mademoiselle." He chuckled, taking her hand. "Perhaps, it's best if you left us in private. My sister and I have much to discuss."

"Oh, I'm sure you do," Marie said with a frown, not being one to take harangue from a male. "But Madeleine has been through enough. Where were you when your sister needed your protection? Smelling spices, smoking pungent cigars, maybe sampling the wares of damsels in distress? Do not throw your accusations. She's not in your control. She has a husband to mind her needs and he's accepted his wife, her lot in life, and loved her well, too."

"I'll kill the bastard when I meet him."

"You're the best friend ever," Madeleine giggled, seeing the humor in the situation. "But perhaps it's best you escaped from our company. I've just found my brother and you'd hurt him without regret." Madeleine grasped her brother's hand. "Marie can shoot a musket, Jean. You best be careful."

He shook his head. "Pretty to boot. Ladies, it's been entertaining."

"Good night," Marie blurted, blushing. She was gone in a flash.

Brother and sister stood mere feet apart, looking at each other over the span of several seconds. Finally, Madeleine fell into his arms, her eyes filling with tears. "Dearest brother, I have faced circumstances that would curdle your milk. I'm grateful, over the moon with gratitude to learn my brother is alive."

"Aye," he agreed, pulling her into his embrace. "And I you, dearest sister. I'm sorry I couldn't help you when you needed me to lean on. Sorry too, I wasn't there in your hour of need."

"Let the past stay buried. I cannot think of that time. I'll tell you about it of course, but for now I want to enjoy my brother's company. Sit, Jean." Madeleine gestured to the chair Marie had just vacated. "Let me pour you a cup of tea."

"I could use a dram of spirits."

"I could ask for the officer to return, make a request?"

"No, tea it will have to be."

They were soon seated, with Madeleine holding her teacup in her hand. "Your travels." She smiled, sipping her tea. "Tell me your stories of passage on the high sea, where you've been and what you've seen."

"So much life. There were times when the weather became so rough, I thought I'd not be able to return. Came close to dying, being swept off the ship."

"I'm grateful you survived the perils of harsh weather. But please continue, I must know everything."

CHAPTER 30

*J*ulian drew the woolen collar of his long-coat upward to protect his ears from the cold. The weather had shifted the past few days while trudging through a forest of emerald-green coniferous trees. He was sure the drop in the temperature had brought the rainwater close to the freezing point, having seen thin sheets of ice collecting on the river.

It was rough being caught outside. The wind emitted a high-pitched whistle that swept through the trees and beat against his face, numbing his flesh and watering his eyes. He had grown a full beard to protect his skin, but the coarse hairs hardly helped.

Scrutinizing gray clouds, he could see how low they hung in the sky. God, how he missed the summer months. Rain began to fall in earnest. Big fat droplets mixed with sleet spat against his face, and then a deluge, a wall of freezing rain, punished his sight. Winter was coming. He could feel the polar winds. Tomorrow, snow would blanket the ground.

Tonight, all he hoped for was to reach Fort Sainte-Anne, his warm bed, and the wife who would join him there.

A few more hours…

"It's a bitch of day," Mack grumbled, pausing, standing beneath the branches of a pine tree. "But if we push hard, we could reach the fort by day's end."

"I hope so. I long for a hot meal, a roaring fire, a warm bed, and…"

"Aye, your wife. I have many days of travel left before I can see Kiah," Mack said with a half-smile, "and our children. They'll have missed their father. I'll leave tomorrow."

"Two more weeks of this weather, more walking on a ground about to freeze? I feel sorry for you. I've asked permission to remain at Fort Sainte-Anne, at least until after the baby's born. My request has been granted."

"And how do you feel about that?"

"About what?"

"About the child, it's not yours. It cannot possibly be…"

"Let me tell you something, my friend. Any boy can fit between a woman's legs, but it takes a real man to father a child. I'm bone-tired, weary to the soul, but if you think to question me on this…"

"No, no," Mack said with a laugh, gripping his shoulder. "I'm glad of your position, and proud of you for stating your case. You've found a good woman. And I'll be the first to bid my welcome to your child."

"I want to be at the fort prior to the child being born. I want to be nearby, should Madeleine need me."

"I'm glad to hear it. I'd bear the waiting period with you, but I long for home and the love I've been missing."

Julian sighed, the rain was finally letting up, enough that they could continue their journey. "Onward, soldiers," he ordered, motioning with his hand, his sword dangling at his side, a musket held in his hands. Mack fell in by his side, keeping pace with him, his company of men taking up the rear.

Everyone was weary, hungry. Julian could see the fatigue in their eyes. He wanted this conflict to be over, his reasons no different than his officers. Peace would come in time, but for now, they must dig deep for strength and make the final push toward home.

"I'm surprised the Mohawk warriors didn't meet us in battle," Mack said, scrutinizing the trees. "It's not their usual style."

"I see what you're thinking. We're not safe yet, they could be stalking us from behind the trees."

"I'm alert to the possibilities, regardless of the weather. Though I hope lessons have been learned after we burned their villages, pillaging whatever we could."

"An unpleasant task. Awful," Julian said earnestly, "a horrible injustice watching a village burn, robbing men of their shelter. Winter is here. Can you imagine not having a home to return to?"

"They're resilient, they'll rebuild. Hopefully better men, stronger men, for the lessons learned."

"Lessons? What did we learn? What did we teach?" Julian replied, shaking his head. "A bastard business. Burning villages before the snow flies. Seems to me, we're no richer for our footsteps across *their* land. If we're ever to coexist and form a lasting peace…"

"It's our land now. We've taken it. That's a hard lesson to learn."

"We've shown them our might, what we're capable of, but men don't change their stance voluntarily."

"Aye, sometimes the transition to peace requires force."

"Mack, I'm too cold to talk, let alone contemplate political give and take. Men will be men, of that I'm sure. One conflict will lead to the next. Put our best foot forward and focus on the ground we must cover. Home. I want to go home."

"Makes me hungry thinking about it."

THE SUN SET EARLY these days. Some evenings, Madeleine watched the sunset; a big ball of orange light sliding beneath the horizon, reveling in the fall colors the colder air seemed to paint. Trees colored with amazing shades of orange and red, and a blue sky stretching on forever, glistening with pink. The sky was breathtakingly beautiful.

On this night, she stood at the gates, gazing across a tall grassy knoll covered with falling snow, searching for any sign of her husband and the officers he led. It had been a month. Even though her brother was here and entertained her company, she missed Julian and her heart ached for him to return.

Where are you?

"Please come back to me," she whispered, taking a deep breath, expelling it with a sigh.

"Come inside," Jean said, approaching where she stood.

"It's cold tonight. Your husband won't return any sooner because you will it. Don't freeze yourself to the bone waiting for him."

She pulled her fur wrap tighter around her shoulders. "You're not my keeper, Jean."

"You're not the same girl I left behind."

She stared at him. "Did you think everything would be the same when you returned home to France? That you'd find your family the way you left them? I grew up while you were at sea. Too fast."

"I can see you have changed," he said sincerely, gazing at her face for once and not her belly. "I cannot change the past."

"You could say you're sorry, for not being there when I needed you."

"Would it have made a difference?"

"Yes. I would have had someone to protect me."

"I don't see how dredging up the past can benefit the future."

"Very well," Madeleine said, seeing her brother was right, even if it hurt. "If you won't say you're sorry, perhaps it's best we go inside."

He offered her his arm. She looked him in the eye, scrutinized his offered arm.

"Come on," he said, "I want to be your security, but I cannot if you will not accept my good intentions." She grasped his arm. "I am sorry, Madeleine."

She glanced at her brother, feeling her belly constrict. "I'm sorry, too. Let's go inside."

"I invited Marie to dine with us tonight."

"She has a husband, Jean. I see the way you look at her."

"Madeleine, I will not accept this kind of impertinence from you. She's lost her husband. She needs a friend."

"She has one. She has me."

"Why are you so angry?"

"I don't know," she said, swallowing. "I suppose I don't feel well tonight."

"The baby?" he asked, as they came closer to her door, her quarters.

"No, I don't think so. If my calculations are correct, I have at least one more month before the child's due."

"You're as big as a manor house." He laughed, opening the door and leading her through. "Either you've grown a strapping lad inside your belly, or you've miscalculated the dates."

Madeleine shook her head. Men. What did they know about expecting a child? But he was right, her tummy was large. When standing, she could not see her feet, was often uncomfortable and had difficulty sleeping at night. She did fear the baby would come into the world before Julian could return home.

"Don't look so worried," her brother said, trying to offer some comfort, "it will soon be over. You look like…"

"I've never done this before, Jean. I have a right to be frightened."

"Come on, mine sister, women have been giving birth since time began."

"Well, that may be true, but…"

Marie entered the chamber. Madeleine saw her vexing expression and worried what she might say. She opened her mouth and took a deep breath as if considering her opinion on the matter. Madeleine waited for yet another clash between friend and brother to begin.

"I see you're the same buxom fellow," Marie said, her cheeks flaming pink, "engaging your sister with kindness and a generous heart."

Madeleine could see her friend was angry, but was her flush brought on from anger or from standing near her brother. Marie closed the door and stepped further inside the room.

"Good evening, Marie," Madeleine said with a smirk, hoping for peace.

"My lady," Jean said, taking Marie's fingers into his hand and kissing them. "You've arrived in time to save us from another quarrel."

"I see," Madeleine said with surprise. So, Marie has taken a fancy to Jean. It was surprising, and too soon. Perhaps it wasn't a war, after all.

Someone knocked at the door. Before Madeleine could make an inquiry, the door opened.

"Oh," she exclaimed, seeing Julian in the doorway. She took in his disheveled appearance, focusing on his hazel eyes. Messy hair and a full beard, he removed his slouch hat into his hands. "Julian," she said, stepping to him. But he wore a strange expression on his face.

"Who is this man?"

"Him?" Madeleine replied, confused, seeing anger banking in her husband's eyes.

"Oh, Julian," she said, rushing to his side. He pulled her

into his arms, his fingers easing into her hair. "Don't fret. This is Jean, my brother Jean."

"You've returned," Marie said, her voice sounding strangled. "Please tell me you bring news of Gauvain?"

"I'm exhausted, must we speak about this now? I'd like to be alone with my wife."

Crestfallen, Marie walked to the door. "Of course."

"Marie…"

"It's all right," Marie flinched, her voice full of sorrow, "your silence says all." She fled from the room.

Jean extended his hand and Julian reluctantly accepted it. "Nice to meet you. I guess this makes us brothers."

Julian merely nodded.

"I'll leave you two in private and see to Marie."

"Good night," Madeleine said, watching Jean take his leave. She turned to her husband, seeing the fatigue in his eyes, and the way he held himself. He grasped her, hugged her briefly, then gazed at her eyes, his lips soon crushing her mouth with a kiss.

"Oh, my darling," he said, his fingers stroking her face. "I'll never leave you again."

"I've waited for you, watched for you every day, every night."

"And how's the baby?" he grinned, placing his hand on her belly.

"I have news on the baby front," she began, feeling a strange wetness between her legs.

"Oh," he said with concern, staring at her strangely.

"My water has broken, Julian. It appears you've arrived home just in time."

CHAPTER 31

"What else can I do?" Julian begged of his wife, squeezing Madeleine's hand. He watched her ever-changing expression, bearing incessant labor pains that had persisted throughout the night. How many hours must she endure? When would this child come into the world? Madeleine, *soon-to-be a mother,* was exhausted from her labors.

He didn't like seeing her this way, her face awash with fear, tears streaming from her eyes, and her breath panting from her sweet lips in quick gasps. Thank heavens; there were pauses in the pathway to motherhood.

"Ah," Madeleine cried out.

He could not take the struggle, or her pain, any longer.

"How do I help, doc?" Julian stared at Jacques Meneu, hoping the surgeon could assist in some way, achieving more than staring at his wife's personal parts. He'd brought the surgeon to the fort to aid in her suffering. What the hell was the man accomplishing and was he fit to assist with the birthing?

"It won't be long," he replied, dismissing the concern, "I can assure you."

"How do you know?"

"The pains, they're coming faster and closer together. Are you sure you want to be here? I've asked you politely to leave the bedchamber, several times over the course of the night. Most men have no stomach for this business. Please wait outside. Marie can fetch you a strong drink."

"The baby…" Madeleine moaned, her nails digging into his palms, bringing his attention back to his wife.

How could he leave? The anguish wrinkled her face with perspiration, but her pains would soon be over. Was he ready for the responsibility? Ready or not, a child would soon be born into the world, and he had promised to be its father. Could he follow through with his promises and a lifetime of responsibility?

"It's all right, ma chérie," he said soothingly, caressing her forehead with his free hand. "This will be over soon."

She stared at him, her amber-brown eyes frosted with fear. She squeezed his hand, holding on so tight to his fingers they were beginning to numb. In the slight pause, the gap between her labors, her breath rasped from her mouth.

"This child will tear me apart."

"Let me check you again," the surgeon said, "it cannot be long now."

Madeleine nodded, searching his expression. "Are you ready for this, Julian? Ready to be a father?"

"I'll stand by you. I promised I would."

"Yes, but what about the child? Tell me, Julian, I need to depend on you."

Not knowing how to respond, Julian turned to the doctor, and watched him examining his wife. There was time to reflect, the baby wasn't here yet.

"Julian!" she screamed, pulling his hand to her chest. "I need to know…"

"It's time," the surgeon declared, "I can see the head. Julian, you must leave the bedchamber. I insist. Now!"

What should he say, what should he do? A baby was coming into the world. His wife bore the pain and yet, he was afraid of the birthing. He released his wife's hand and stepped away as the doctor had instructed.

"Tell me you're ready for this," Madeleine moaned, "my baby's coming into the world. I cannot do this alone."

Retreating, he scrutinized her expression, seeing her pain and worry. He would accept the commitment. Risks must be shared. "Our baby," he said, hoping he sounded sincere, walking closer to the door, "you're not alone."

"Get out of here, Julian. Push!" the surgeon said. "Bring this baby into the world."

Julian stood at the threshold, hearing his wife groaning, not wanting to leave her, his hand on the doorframe. Jean grasped his arm and pulled him from the room. He felt helpless.

"Julian—" Madeleine screamed.

He fought against Jean's grip, wanting to be with his wife, but her brother would not permit his re-entry. "I won't go inside," he grumbled, shrugging against the hold, glaring at his brother-in-law.

"Push," the doctor urged. "You can do this. You can bring this child into the world."

"Ah," she cried out, one final time. A wail of a cry broke forth, and Julian turned toward the sound, seeing a baby in the doctor's hands. The surgeon broke into a smile, the first sign of emotion Julian had seen on his face.

"It's a boy," Jacques Meneu said, placing the baby on Madeleine's tummy, "parents, you have a son."

"We have a son," Julian said, gazing at his wife, gazing at the child bawling against her breast. Tiny fingers. Tiny toes. Small and helpless; how could a man fear such perfection? He wanted to return to his wife's side, wanted to see his son up close.

"May I come back inside the room?" Julian asked of Jacques Meneu, hoping.

"No. Go have a drink. When mother and child have been attended to and are in a presentable condition, only then may you return. Jean?" the surgeon asked of Madeleine's brother, appearing serious again. "Close the door."

Jean did as the doctor requested. "This is a nasty business. I don't know why you're so determined to watch it."

"Don't start with me," Julian said, marching straight for the cabinet to retrieve a dram of cognac. "One day, I promise you, men will not be relegated to the borders of the parenting bed."

"The next thing you'll tell me is men will travel to the moon. Quite unlikely."

"We'll see about space travel, too," Julian stated, passing Jean a cut-glass beaker, then filling it. "Cheers, to my son."

"Cheers indeed. You're a good man, Julian. I appreciate your care of my sister and her child."

"Our child, and don't you ever forget it."

IN THE PERIOD between night and the morning sunrise, Julian lay beside his wife in their bed. Bone-tired from his journey home, he should have slept. Instead, he gazed at the baby boy nestled in his arms. Sound asleep, the little lad seemed the most precious gift he had ever held in his arms.

"Your mother is sleeping," he said, smiling. "But we need this time together, you and me. You see, your mother has held you close all these months. Now, it's my turn."

The child made a tiny mewing sound.

"I'm not your real father," Julian said, sighing, wondering why he revealed this information to a baby who would not understand. "And this is the only moment I'll share this news, for my love for you is all that matters. I make you this promise, I will hold you close, keep you warm, care for you, see that you're well fed, and assist you to grow into a responsible lad. Maybe change your nappy," Julian said, chuckling, stroking the baby's face. "We'll call you Michel. After my father."

"That's kind of you, Julian. But will your father recognize our son?"

"Look who's awake," Julian cooed, smiling at his new son and his wife. "This is between Michel and me, my darling wife. But you're welcome to share your opinion."

She was exhausted, even after her brief rest, but she smiled. "Oh, you're having a conversation?"

"Yes. Our son requires a name."

"And you think Michel would be a good choice?"

"I do."

"How would your father feel about this boy, having his name? Would you rather save this designation," she paused, he could see the exasperation in her eyes, "for your son?"

Julian knew what his wife was trying to say, and he thanked her for it, but he had to make a commitment. "Madeleine, I want my first child to have my father's name. Please."

"Who am I to stand between a father and his son? If this is your wish, let it be so. Michel Xavier Benoit."

"Xavier?"

"It's a saint name; it means new house. I want our child to have such a middle name, for him, for us, as we begin a new life, together."

"And what do you think of this, little one," Julian mused, reflecting on the name. "Seems a big name for one of little size."

"May I hold, Michel?" Madeleine said tenderly, beseeching, staring at him, wonderment in her eyes.

"Must I give him up so soon?"

Julian passed the boy into his wife's arms. His son was soon suckling at her breast.

Madeleine stared at her husband, a certain hunger, desire in her eyes. "As long as I live, I'll never forget this moment. I love you for it, Julian Benoit. Your care of me, your care of our son."

Julian leaned in close, threading his fingers through her hair. "Aw, chérie, I love you too. With all of my heart."

After a time, Julian laid his head on the pillow. Madeleine drew her fingers through his hair, her fingertips massaging his scalp. He closed his eyes, welcoming her touch and soon succumbed to sleep while listening to suckling sounds and dreaming of a shared life together. He was grateful; grateful Madeleine Bourbonnais had had the courage to journey to this new world.

A heart from across the ocean was his to have and to hold for as long they both should live, and he was glad of it.

EPILOGUE

*M*arie closed the door to Julian and Madeleine's quarters to give the new family their privacy. Standing next to the log building and breathing the frosty night air, she wrapped her shawl around her shoulders and stared at the black velvet sky. Big puffy swirls of snow began to fall. *Amazing!* She had never witnessed the mystery of winter or the swirl of snowflakes before. She stuck out her tongue, hoping to catch a flake.

"How are they?" Jean Bourbonnais asked of her, coming to stand by her side.

"Mother and child are fine," she said with a grimace, wishing Madeleine's brother would leave her to contemplate her thoughts in private.

"I can see you're unhappy to see me," he said, coming closer, "but can you at least tell me how the child is faring?"

"Hmm," she snorted, studying him.

Marie didn't like Jean, perhaps because he had left his sister and his family, and she blamed him for her friend's life struggles. It was his fault to some extent that this trouble had befallen Madeleine, and she was her best friend. She owed Maddie her loyalty. But the child came to mind, the sweet baby, and she smiled.

"He's doing well." She finally relented, telling him. "A beautiful little son. Ten fingers. Ten toes."

"You say that as if you'd like to have one, too."

"Why are you here, Jean?"

"I see the way you look at me. You think I have no care of my sister? No compassion for the trials she's been through? I traveled across the ocean, from France to find her."

"And now that you've found her, what will you do? Leave her again? Travel back to France across the same stretch of water?"

"Why do you dislike me, Marie? What have I done to put my good name in low esteem?"

Marie studied his expression, scrutinizing the man who stared at her as if her response mattered. Normally, she'd react with a tart retort, a quick reply, but she saw no reason why she should not at least consider friendship.

"I don't know," she replied, responding honestly.

"Marie Chauvet, you and I have begun our friendship on unequal footing. You think I abandoned my sister. I did nothing of the sort. I would like to begin this relationship again. Will you hear me out?"

Marie looked at Jean, her facial expression softening, her cheeks warming. "I could be urged to see reason. Perhaps, we could share a nightcap, together? If you promise to be a gentleman and respect the fact I'm a married woman."

He offered her his arm. She gazed at his strength,

wondering if she should accept his grasp. She remembered Gauvain and frowned. Missing him. Missing his strength, intimacy and companionship. Not really a love match, their time together had been short, more so human warmth shared through a sexual nature. It had been good.

What would her husband think if he could see where her emotions strayed to now, contemplating Jean, in a sensual way? Who was she kidding; her husband was dead.

"Don't worry, beautiful woman," Jean said, interrupting her reverie. "We'll talk of adventure and the journeys I have experienced at sea. I'll tell you why I left my family—what I hoped to find—and if you should succumb to other pleasures, I promise you this, they'll be enjoyable."

"You sound like a gambler, like the father before you."

"Ah," he laughed, snickering. "*The Treasures found at Sea.* I'll tell you about the spoils of trade, too!"

THANK you for reading *A Heart across the Ocean.* If you enjoyed Julian and Madeleine's love story, your honest opinion of their romance will support the author's writing career. Please rate or review this book on your favorite book site, review site, blog, or your own social media properties, and share your opinion with other readers. Thank you!

CONTACT SHELLEY KASSIAN

If you would like to learn more about Shelley or her novels, visit her website at shelleykassian.com. Here you can read excerpts from her books, linked reviews, blog posts, as well as discovering her professional affiliations and accreditation.

Shelley enjoys hearing from her readers. If you'd like to contact the author, send her a message at: shelleykassian@gmail.com.

FOLLOW SHELLEY ON SOCIAL MEDIA

amazon.com/author/shelleykassian

bookbub.com/authors/shelley-kassian

goodreads.com/shelleykassian

facebook.com/ShelleyKassian

instagram.com/shelleykassian

twitter.com/@shelleykassian

pinterest.com/shelleykassian

ABOUT SHELLEY KASSIAN

Bestselling author Shelley Kassian has been writing timeless love stories filled with romance or dark fantasy (romantasy) for more than twenty years, novels that include her recent true love story, *A Mountain Leads Home*. A history enthusiast, she's traveled far and wide to explore secret gardens and medieval castles, having an avid interest in the Tudor period. Her prose has been described as "near rhapsodic," "pitch perfect," and "stylishly straightforward, rarely relying on complex turns of phrase." Reviewers have said her narrative conveys "imaginative fantasy," "fascinating characters," and "refreshing romance."

Shelley's taken creative writing courses, holds board positions within professional associations, and retains a Professional Editing Certificate. Drawing on her expertise, she has mentored novice writers, but her passion comes alive while scribing her stories into novel-length fiction. Shelley shares her life with her husband, adores her adult children and two grand pups, and when not relaxing at her seaside cottage, lives in Calgary, Alberta, Canada.

www.ingramcontent.com/pod-product-compliance
Lightning Source LLC
Chambersburg PA
CBHW031944130726
47905CB00002BA/508